"I'm not asking for any commitments or promises, Brett." Kirsten ran a hand through Brett's hair and down Brett's face. Brett moved her hands up Kirsten's body, feeling the swell of her tits, enjoying the silkiness of the naked skin. Kirsten breathed deeply, bringing more attention to her breasts. Brett ran her hands down over the outsides of her thighs.

"Right here and now, baby, right here and now," Kirsten said as she pulled Brett's face to her breast. Brett eagerly clamped onto the nipple, sucking it, lightly biting it, teasing it with her tongue. Kirsten moaned her appreciation. Brett pulled her roughly into her, pressing her belt buckle into Kirsten's wet pussy.

"Ooo, yes," she said as Brett picked her up and put her on the desk. Brett ran her hands roughly up and down her body as she arched in pleasure. Kirsten guided Brett's hands to her pussy where Brett ran her fingers roughly up and down the swollen, wet lips. "I want you inside me."

Brett shoved four fingers into her, trying to play rough, but Kirsten moaned and arched again, whimpering until Brett pushed her entire fist into her, pulling it in and out and twisting it around, while her other hand roughly twisted and pulled on first one then the other nipple.

"That's it baby, I like it rough, ride me hard, baby."

WHEN THE DANCING STOPS

The First Brett Higgins Mystery

THERESE
SZYMANSKI

THE NAIAD PRESS, INC.
1997

Printed in the United States of America on acid-free paper
First Edition

Editor: Christine Cassidy
Cover designer: Bonnie Liss (Phoenix Graphics)
Typesetter: Sandi Stancil

Library of Congress Cataloging-in-Publication Data

Szymanski, Therese, 1968 –
When the dancing stops : a Brett Higgins mystery / by Therese Szymanski
p. cm.
"First in a series of lesbian mysteries featuring Brett Higgins" — Data sheet.
ISBN 1-56280-186-4 (pbk.)
I. Title.
PS3569.Z94W48 1997
813′.54—dc21 97-10804
CIP

This is for all the women who have loved, nurtured, taught, cared for and inspired me:

Especially Jacquie, Cheryl, Stacy, Andy, Mick, Phyllis, Sheila, Dawn, Terri, Lessa, Virginia, Carol K., C.J.H., Sharon B., Carol and Carol, Aphrodite, Jennifer, Nicki B., Julia, Jillian, Kay, Donna, Jan, Courtney and Laura and Kathy.

About the Author

Therese Szymanski is an award-winning playwright who works in advertising and plays in theatre — with both *POW* (*Pissed Off Wimmin*) and *Alternating Currents*. She enjoys hanging around in extremely unsavory neighborhoods (including the Cass Corridor), or dancing and cruising at the Railroad Crossing. She has never been accused of political correctness and finds most of her past too strange to share with anyone until at least the second date.

She has lived all her life in the Detroit area.

Prologue

Cold rain, threatening an early Michigan winter, pelted her as she got out of her car and walked to the nearby gathering. The wind whipped through the trees, making them dance to its own bizarre tune while leaves were blown from limbs to scuttle across clearings. The sky above boiled while dark clouds fought one another in an ongoing battle of dominance. No winner was in sight.

It was the sort of dreary, early fall day that should have been spent in front of a roaring fire with a lover, a soft blanket, a bear rug, a bottle of champagne and a bowl of strawberries. She no longer had any of that. She shivered and pulled her coat closer. The darkness of the day matched her mood.

The cemetery was cold and gray as she stood just outside the huddled ring of people, wondering if they knew she was the one who had pulled the trigger. She pulled her hat a bit lower.

A tall woman with dark hair and a black umbrella was speaking, and the words floated across the clearing like smoke. "Although some try to say otherwise, she was a good person . . ."

A cold gust of wind blew across the clearing and she pulled her coat closer, fervently hoping no one recognized her. She stared at the coffin being lowered into the ground and a cloud of emotion, darker than any on this cold and uncaring day, swept over her like a rag. Too young to die, she thought to herself, too much left to do and say . . .

"Ashes to ashes, and dust to dust . . ."

The few moments it took to end a life were chiseled onto her mind like the lettering on the tombstone. When she closed her eyes she again felt the cold steel of the gun in her hand, heard the blast as the shots rang out, felt the pull of the recoil. She saw the body crumple into a pool of blood. Angry lightning had flashed through the night sky. She saw the dream of what could have been die with the woman she loved. The only woman she could ever truly love.

She shivered as her heart tightened, as the tears ran from her eyes. She shook with the pain that would forever be hers. She was sad, hurt and vengeful; but most of all, she was filled with regret.

PART ONE:
FRIENDS AND FOES

CHAPTER 1
The Dance Begins

It was the early '90s and the Democrats had just taken control of the U.S. legislature. Bush still chose the decor of the Oval Office, and a storm was brewing in the deserts half a world away. All of this made no difference to Rick DeSilva and Brett Higgins, who met at Six Mile and Woodward in Detroit — Motown, the Motor City, the Murder Capital of the World. All that mattered to them was the bottom line.

The building they met in was decorated with a

frieze that proclaimed it had once housed the Highland Park National Bank. Now it was home to an adult theater, an escort service, and a pornography distributor and held the offices of Rick, Brett and Frankie Lorenzini, the people who ran those businesses, as well as a few others. Rick was the owner, worried mostly about expanding the businesses, Brett was the advertising/marketing head and general manager, and Frankie took care of problems.

Rick looked up as Brett entered his office and poured herself a drink. He reached underneath his desk and brought forth a black leather briefcase, which he slammed down and opened for Brett's inspection. Brett leaned against the large oak desk, which he had bought when he first took over the business, saying that no real work could be accomplished on the old stainless steel one his father had used.

"There it is, fifty grand, all in twenties," Rick said, standing and crossing his arms in front of his lean frame. At only 5′10″ and 165 pounds, Rick preferred to show his power through his actions and possessions rather than his size. He always dressed immaculately in expensive suits with silk ties, fashioning himself after a rich businessman, because that was what he imagined himself to be. "Twenty-five hundred little pieces of green paper."

"For a few million particles of dust." Brett leafed through the cash, liking the feel of the money and the way it looked, situated all nice and neat in the case. "And I always thought Ralph just liked the dancers." She pulled out the engraved Zippo a woman had once given her and with one hand expertly opened it, flipped a flame and lit her Marlboro.

"He does. But he also likes the cash. Being a cop don't pay much."

"And who better to get the shit through Detroit Metro?"

"I really don't give a rat's ass how they beef up airport security — if the right people have a good enough reason to get it through, it gets through."

Brett took a sip of her Glenfiddich single malt scotch and walked over to the window to gaze at the grim day and the busy street below. Woodward at Six Mile — no one ever referred to streets anywhere in the metropolitan area with "Street" or "Boulevard" or "Avenue" — was corroded with potholes, bordered by burnt buildings, broken pay phones, abandoned buildings and a few working but disreputable convenience stores and laundromats. Some said Detroit was making a comeback, but she didn't think it was possible. Detroit had always relied on the auto-makers for its sustenance, but now the cars were being manufactured overseas, leaving Detroit a mere has-been of a city. Rick came up behind her.

"As long as they demand, we'll get the supply," she said.

"That something you learned in college?" Rick asked, frowning at a splotch on the window.

"Sort of," Brett replied as Rick cleaned the smudge.

Frankie Lorenzini, a big man at 6′6″ and 275 pounds who looked every bit of his Italian heritage, entered the room and gazed at them with sleepy eyes. He grabbed the briefcase, slammed it shut and handed it to Brett.

"You goin' anywhere from here?" Frankie asked.

"Just to the rap group in Ferndale," Brett replied.

"Storm's been askin' 'bout you."

"That so?" Brett checked herself out in the mirror, quickly smoothing her hair back. She had just changed from her work clothes into black Levi's men's 550 jeans and a black T-shirt. She picked up her well-worn black leather jacket and flipped it over her shoulder.

"Maybe you should stop by and say hello." Rick buttoned the jacket on his tailored suit. "Frankie'll watch the case." He escorted them from his office, locking the door behind him.

The trio headed down the stairs. Frankie and Brett headed into the theater and Rick went off for a meeting about other forms of business. He was always interested in expansion.

CHAPTER 2
Allie

Allie climbed into her dusty blue Geo Prizm and silently hoped the rain wouldn't turn into snow. She thought about the end of the fall and how it was like the end to a chapter of her life. She hoped the next chapter would be better than the last.

She hung a right onto Big Beaver and headed west, toward Woodward. She wondered if I-75 would be a better route to take, but she didn't want to risk getting stuck in the evening rush hour traffic. She was a bit nervous tonight; she didn't want to be late because this was the first time she was going to the women's rap group at Affirmations, the local LesBiGay Community Center. Up until now she had only gone to their youth group.

At 17, Allison Sullivan had always been her daddy's little kitten — pretty, cute, shy. She loved her father, who was a design engineer at General Motors. He had given her the Prizm for her Sweet 16, wanting her to know he trusted her and realized she was old enough to start having greater independence.

John and Maggie Sullivan had all but given up hopes of ever having children when Maggie became pregnant with Allie. When he was younger, John wanted both a son and a daughter, but he was thankful when Allie was born free from defects and that Maggie came through it all right as well. They had been worried, as they were both in their early forties by the time Maggie got pregnant, and there is a great deal of danger in having a first child that late in life.

Allie loved her parents, and wanted to be everything they wanted her to be, but then, exactly one year ago, Allie's best friend Cybill told her she was a lesbian. Then came that fateful Saturday, when she woke up all alone in the house — her parents were at the mall. She walked into the bathroom and looked into the mirror: full lips; a small, dainty nose; long, wavy, golden hair that had covered the faces of so many guys as she lay upon them; clear, deep blue eyes; a sexy 5′8″ near-model body that guys seemed to want with its long legs and tiny waist.

She looked into the mirror, took a deep breath

and said the words too long denied and delayed: "Allie, you are a lesbian."

And it felt good, it felt right. But Cybill didn't see it that way.

"No, Allie, you're just confused," Cybill had said later that evening as she calmly sipped her wine at the dining room table in her apartment. The dinner dishes lay scattered around them.

"I am not confused!"

"You just see the fun we have . . ."

"It has nothing to do with you — this is about me."

"Don't let me be a role model to that extent."

"Why can't you, of all people, understand that this is just the way I am?"

"Allie . . ."

"Some friend you are — first you come out, and then you can't understand it when I do!" Allie cried as she ran from the apartment. She was hurt when Cybill didn't follow. She never found out what Cybill was thinking and feeling that night.

Thank God for Erin, though. Cybill apparently felt so guilty about Allie's "delusions," she told her 21-year-old girlfriend Erin about it, and Erin was the one who gave Allie a shoulder to lean on. She also introduced her to the youth group at Affirmations. That was what became her true life preserver in the storm to follow. Of course, that was also where she first met Kirsten.

She had driven by the building which housed the group several times, on several different weekends, before she screwed up the courage to enter.

She snuck into the group and looked around,

trying to go unnoticed. There were about fifteen guys, and only five other women, and all of them were greeting one another with hugs and kisses, regardless of sex. Before she could find a corner to crawl into, a woman with shoulder-length auburn hair walked up to her. Although she wasn't the most gorgeous woman Allie had ever seen, there was something sensual and sexy about her.

"Hi, stranger," she said. And Allie remembered, to this day, with some embarrassment, that the first thing she noticed about Kirsten were her tits.

"Uh, hi," Allie nervously replied to the floor. Dirt was ingrained into the worn tiles, becoming a part of the pattern.

"This your first time here?"

"Yeah, how'd you know?"

"You look like you wanna run the hell out of here."

"Oh." Allie felt a blush rise up to her cheeks.

"C'mon, you can sit next to me." Kirsten took Allie's hand and led her to two vacant seats. Allie knew everything was going to be all right.

As it turned out, everything was more than all right. The first time Allie kissed Kirsten, she knew for sure. The softness of those lips, the gentleness no guy could ever match, the feeling of another woman's body pressed against hers . . . It all added up — the soft, melodic voice, the smooth legs, and the chest that was so like a pillow after sex — now it all made sense, these were the things that turned her on, that made her melt. Allie finally knew why men loved women as much as they did.

Allie wanted a relationship just like her parents

had — lasting, loving, nurturing. She wanted to build both a home and a life with someone, a life that would endure through the hard times and shine during the good.

Kirsten, a senior at Cousino High School in Warren, had been out since she was fourteen. She shared her firsthand knowledge about being gay with Allie, showing her how two women communicated, where to meet other lesbians and how to interact with the community as a whole. Kirsten made Allie feel important, wanted. She was good for Allie, in the beginning at least. Until Allie found out more about her.

Kirsten liked things her way; everything had to be just so. They dated for three months, and although they had never discussed monogamy, Allie had heard of an unwritten lesbian code that said one should only date one woman at a time. Apparently no one ever told Kirsten this.

At first she thought it was just rumors spread by jealous people who had no one. Then she began to pay attention and started to notice a pattern to the times Kirsten wasn't available, realized that Kirsten avoided conversations about what she did when she wasn't in school, at work or with Allie. When Allie confronted her on the subject, she skillfully denied it. She denied it throughout their entire break-up, then plied Allie with gifts and attention, trying to win her back.

"You know," Kirsten said a few weeks later when they ran into each other at group. "We coulda had it so good."

"We can still be friends."

"I'm willing to give you another chance."

"Give me another chance? I don't need another chance. You were the one that screwed up."

"That was only until I realized how much you meant to me," Kirsten replied, always quick on her feet and with her tongue. In more ways than one.

"How much I meant to you? That only became apparent when you knew I was outta there."

"All those other women meant nothing . . ."

"So you finally admit you were cheating on me."

"That's not what I meant."

"You sound just like a man!" Allie headed for the exit.

"Allison!" Kirsten called. Allie looked at her. "You don't know loneliness like you'll know if you walk out that door."

Allie felt like her best friend had just killed her dog. Intentionally.

It was all of that that led Peggy, one of Affirmations' youth group facilitators, to suggest that Allie might want to try going to the women's rap group instead. She thought Allie was mature enough to fit in and would only be further hurt by continued contact with Kirsten, and Allie definitely wanted to keep going to Affirmations, because she always felt like she belonged there.

With Tina, Allie thought she found it all: looks, common interests, brains and a cute ass. They had both tested the waters and felt good about becoming serious, or so she thought, and she even entertained notions of settling down with Tina, or at least she had until two weeks ago, when she decided to pay a surprise visit to Tina. And surprise it was, for both of them. Maybe for all three of them, but then again, maybe not.

Allie had walked into Tina's bedroom to find Tina with her face buried between Kirsten's naked thighs.

Especially during the past week, as she nursed both her broken heart and ego, Allie found solace in imagining herself in uniform. She knew her parents wanted her to go to college, get an education and go on to be a white-collar worker, maybe even a doctor or lawyer, but she couldn't picture herself as a desk jockey; she had too much energy and loved people too much for that. Plus she also knew her father wouldn't retire until she finished school, so she wouldn't get an advanced degree.

There had been cops in her family for as long as she could remember — her grandpa and Uncle Jack. She thought it was about time a woman joined. She remembered the way people looked at her grandpa, the respect and admiration they gave him, she gave him, and she imagined people looking at her that way — seeing beyond her hair, face and body and respecting her both for her accomplishments and what she could do.

People would learn to take her seriously.

CHAPTER 3
Brett

Storm walked along the wall to the stage as the men hooted and hollered and the slow, agonizing, almost religious music of Enigma filled the auditorium. Pictures on the huge screen cast strange, flickering lights upon the audience and the stage lights cast light and shadow across Storm's body, making her slightly olive-colored skin all the more exotic. She walked onstage in her small, tight red dress and threw her long black hair back over her shoulders, boldly staring with dark eyes across the rows of seated men, as diverse in their skin color as they were alike in their appetites.

She started moving to the music and the men quieted. Her movements were slow, subtle and sexy — sexy as she inched her thin skirt up to display shapely legs clad in stiletto heels and fishnet stockings, sexy as she pulled her top down just enough to reveal the curves of her full breasts. Her job was sex, and she did her job well.

In the darkness of the auditorium, with its black walls and floors, cigarette-burnt seats and sticky floor, Storm spun, strutted and stretched, revealing her body slowly, bit by bit, for the admiration of the drooling men in the audience. She danced not for the men, but for herself.

It was into this murkiness that Brett came. She looked about, adjusting to the sudden darkness, listening to the heavy breathing of the men as they released their ever swelling members from the tight restraints of their pants. But it was the smell that was the worst, the smell of sweat and filth and urine and semen, the smell of stale cigarette smoke and new cigarette smoke, the smell of men in their most primal state.

Brett sat in the center of the auditorium where the nearest client was several seats from her and looked to the stage, where Storm danced for herself.

Storm pulled down the top of her dress to reveal her luscious breasts in their entirety. She licked her lips and stretched, still moving to the music, as she slowly looked over the audience until she found Brett.

Her dark eyes met Brett's and she smiled a soft, sultry, knowing smile. She stepped out of the dress and casually tossed it to the side.

Wearing only fishnets, g-string and heels, she didn't dance for the men, she didn't dance for herself, she danced for Brett. As she spread her legs, to hint at the secrets there, as she fondled her smooth breasts and excited the nipples even more, as she moved to the music and thrust her hips out, as she slid her g-string off, she did it for Brett.

When she tossed her g-string to Brett, Brett deftly caught it and smiled, then brought it up to her nose to inhale the intoxicating scent. She slowly smiled as Storm turned and spread her legs, legs that Brett imagined wrapped around her waist, wrapped around her neck.

Storm ran her hands over her body, stopping to tease the nearly bursting nipples, before she opened the lips of her pussy and spread her legs wider still. She dipped the tip of her finger into her own juices and slowly brought it up to her lips to lick it like a lollipop.

The beat of the music became her heartbeat and the beat played on. All that existed were Storm and Brett and the music. The music that swelled and filled the air like static electricity, with its beat that controlled their groins, pulsating their cunts like a lapping tongue.

The song ended. Storm strutted, proud in her body, proud in her nakedness, to the control panel to dim the lights. And as Brett stood to leave, Storm walked up to her.

"I believe you have something of mine." Storm's

voice was husky as she pushed her thick hair back over her shoulders.

"And what will you give me for it?"

"What would you like?" She wrapped her arms around Brett's neck and pressed her naked body into Brett's.

Brett slid her hands around Storm's waist, pulling her crotch in to touch her own, and as the next song started, as the next beat invaded their universe, Storm and Brett stood, melded as one, in a room full of men.

"This one's on the house," Storm murmured in Brett's ear as she pushed her into the seat and sat on her lap.

Brett knew the dancers were supposed to wear a g-string when performing lap dances, but this was a special lap dance given only for her.

Storm swayed on Brett's lap, her arms around Brett's shoulders, and the beat played on. Strange images on the screen cast weird lights throughout the auditorium. Brett ran her hands over Storm's body, examining her curves, touching the tender skin behind her knees, enjoying the softness of her breasts and the hardness of her nipples. Brett buried her face in the bountiful flesh of Storm's breasts and ran her tongue over Storm's nipples.

Storm groaned and pushed Brett's hands between her legs. "I want you."

"And what if you can't have me?" Brett teased, pulling Storm's mouth to her own while Storm wrapped her long legs around Brett's waist. Brett shoved Storm's back against the seat in front of them as Storm's moans increased.

Brett's fingers explored Storm's wetness, expert in finding just what they sought as they opened Storm to the chilly air. Brett toyed with her; she flicked the hardened clit back and forth while the men around them merely pretended to watch the movie where people fucked like minks but never looked like they enjoyed it.

And the beat played on as Brett bit Storm's nipples. Her fingers grasped the place of being and pulled, flicked and teased.

Not one man failed to notice Storm's moans as every part of her body tightened and she came.

When Brett left the auditorium, Frankie was standing in the entry smiling at her. "Didja have fun?"

"I always have fun," Brett said coolly, licking her fingers. "Where's the case?"

"Right here."

Brett left the building, walked around the corner, climbed into her black Ford Probe and took off, heading north on Woodward to the weekly lesbian rap group at Affirmations, which she tried to make once a month.

Brett was the youngest of seven children, the only girl. Her mother never wanted a girl, because girls only grew up to relive the horror of their mothers' lives. Thus, Alice Higgins turned the other way when her husband and sons beat and abused the young Brett. Although Brett was haunted by nightmares, the only thing she'd ever tell anyone about her childhood was that it gave her strength and the will to succeed. She fought hard through high school, excelling in her classes while maintaining two jobs so she could pay for college, even if she couldn't get a scholarship. She wanted to get out of the house and away from her family.

Her bachelor's degree in business from Michigan State University had led her to her position as Rick DeSilva's first lieutenant. It had been a strange journey, but at 23 she was right hand to the mogul of porn in the Motor City, supervising not only the House of Kinsey, Rick's LesBiGay book and gift store, but also Rick's adult theater, eight adult bookstores, phone sex service, escort service and distribution service, which supplied the surrounding areas with magazines, toys, videos and a few other items. Plus, she had a hand in his more creative enterprises as well. She found her job fun, challenging and interesting. She liked hopping from one activity to another — one minute she'd be taking care of deposits or tracking inventory and sales, discovering what the diverse men who came into these places wanted, from the dancers to the products, and a little later she'd be on the street or in a bar somewhere recruiting a new dancer or escort.

Brett noticed flashing lights behind her. She swore, pulled over and watched as the officer approached.

"Do you know how fast . . ." he began.

"Hey, Ralph!" Brett said to the regular Paradise Theater patron, whom she was to meet with later that night.

"Shit, Brett — if I'd known it was you, I woulda called for backup."

Brett laughed as she mimicked him. " 'Attention, this is Ralph. I'm in hot pursuit of a dyke doin' five miles over the speed limit. Request backup.' "

"Five miles? Try twenty-five! And there's no tellin' what all you got in this piece of shit . . ."

"Few dildos, coupla magazines — nothin' that's illegal in this town."

"How 'bout your gun? Or maybe some drugs?"

"So, Ralph, how's the wife?"

A few minutes later Brett was again heading north on Woodward. As she pulled into the parking lot across from Affirmations she glanced at her watch and realized she was a bit later than she had planned. She hurriedly ran her hands through her hair, grabbed a bottle of cologne from the glove compartment and spritzed herself. She reflexively checked around before she climbed out of the car with the briefcase, which she locked in the trunk before setting the alarm.

Affirmations was located in Ferndale, a small community just north of Detroit where the crime rate was so low she had once seen three police cars show up to investigate dog food grand theft — someone had stolen three bags of dog food from a local grocery store.

Eight Mile was the demarcation line between Detroit and its neighboring suburbs. On the south side of the road was the #1 murder city in the U.S., and to the north were all of the nice places to live. An old joke was that signs on northbound roads heading out of Detroit said "Last one out, turn off the lights," because no one really lived there. This pissed Brett off, because even though she had worked hard to get out, she was born and raised in the city.

In Ferndale Brett wasn't worried about the safety of her Probe. If she drove a Jag or a Porsche, she might, but that was the reason she'd bought the inconspicuous Ford.

Shortly after she moved back to town after college she had come to Affirmations, to one of the multifarious rap groups the center had, and had had to search first for the poorly marked building, then for the exact room where the meeting was hidden. Now she quickly crossed the street to the red brick building, noticing along the way A Woman's Prerogative, the new women's bookstore, just a few doors down. She made a mental note to check out the competition sometime soon.

She walked quickly under the dirty red canopy, opened the glass door to the old building and energetically leapt up two flights of squeaky stairs to the meeting.

The fairly large, well-lit room was warm from the fifty women jammed together in a rough circle. Brett shrugged off her black leather jacket and took one of the last vacant seats, which was just outside the circle in a corner.

A tall, good-looking woman entered. Brett noted her long, blond hair, which fell like a halo about her head. She had a slender figure and wore a leather bomber's jacket, brightly patterned silk shirt and khaki dress slacks. Brett held her breath and smiled when the woman spotted the empty chair near hers.

For the rest of the meeting, Brett kept glancing

at this stranger who looked out of place and nervous amidst the group. She was over-dressed, as if she were trying to prove something. Even Brett had changed out of her normal attire — a man's suit with a silk shirt and tie. As soon as the meeting was over and everyone stood in preparation to depart, Brett looked at the woman. Or, that was the game plan — but somehow she had vanished and some other woman was launching herself at Brett.

"Hi! I'm Shelly!"

"I'm Brett."

"So, what'd you think of the discussion?"

Who was paying attention? "It was, ah, interesting."

"I just think it's so exciting that the Democrats have control of the House and Senate . . ."

Someone yelled her name and grabbed Brett from behind. Brett turned around just in time to catch Denise, who leapt into the air and wrapped her legs around Brett's waist, hugging her tight. Brett laughed and swung Denise around in a circle before landing her back on the ground. She took both Denise's hands in her own and stepped back for a long, appreciative look at bobbed, brown hair, trim figure and twinkling eyes. Denise hadn't changed much at all since that lustful first term at college.

"Oooo! You are so-o-o butch!" Denise squealed in delight as she gave Brett a big hug and Brett lifted her off the floor again.

Shelly cleared her throat.

"Shit," Brett whispered into Denise's ear, putting her back on the floor. "You've got to save me."

Denise pulled Brett's mouth to her own, saying, "You gotta kiss for me, lover?" Brett was all too willing to oblige, and while they reacquainted themselves, Shelly wandered off to make another new friend.

"Almost as good as I remember," Brett said.

" 'Almost?' "

"You must be losing it in your old age."

"Honey, I lost it long ago."

"Many will testify to that."

"I should get you for that."

"You had me long ago."

"Not that long ago," Denise said as she wrapped her arms around Brett's neck. Over the years, Brett wondered if she and 'Nise had done the right thing by breaking up, but even though she still loved her as a friend, she knew they had.

"Hey, watch out." Brett pushed Denise away as her mystery woman returned. "I'm cruising someone else."

Brett noticed the woman's long, curly blond hair, aristocratic nose and long legs — legs long enough to wrap around her waist twice. She smiled to herself as Shelly launched herself at the woman, who shyly tried to pull away while she looked over at Brett, who could only stare into her clear, piercing blue eyes. Brett suddenly realized they were almost the same height — something Brett was not accustomed to at 5′10″. Brett felt her knees go weak.

"Breathe." Denise stood by Brett's side, then said, "Let's take a walk." She took Brett by the arm and led her across the room.

"Excuse me," Denise began, cutting off Shelly's barrage. "But my name's Denise and this is my friend Brett and she would really like to commit a felony with you."

Brett playfully punched Denise's shoulder, Shelly turned red and bustled off, and the blond's jaw dropped before she burst out in laughter.

"Should I be pissed or glad that you got rid of that woman?" she said.

"I'm gonna . . ." Brett began, but Denise glanced at her watch and cut her off.

"Oh my! Will you look at the time? I've just got to get home!" Denise said with a smirk, quickly heading for the door.

"Denise!"

"Is your friend always so blatant?" the woman asked, carefully eyeing Brett's slender, muscular frame up and down.

"My friend is gonna die real soon."

The woman leaned in close and in a throaty whisper murmured, "Does that mean you don't want to fuck me?"

Brett dropped her jacket.

CHAPTER 4
Kirsten

Kirsten had been working up a sweat all night at Backstreet. God! How she loved to dance! She lived for the beat of the music and the sea of admiring faces. She loved the flashing lights, the smell of the hot, sweaty bodies, the music almost tangible in the air. Not for her the humdrum blandness of the everyday world. Not for her the unending swarm of customers she could never quite please. She knew she was meant to have admiring faces following her.

Since the day Kirsten had first stepped out of the closet she had met women only to leave them by the wayside. Beautiful, sexy, intelligent women waited for her long gazes, her sultry smile, her cocked head and jaunty stance. Kirsten had danced from partner to partner, woman to woman, thinking only of herself, not really caring about the promises she made or the hearts she broke. After all, it was in her — her father had left her mother for a younger woman, and Kirsten had been bounced back and forth between her dad and his new wife, and her mother and her many boyfriends. Nothing in this life was meant to last, she thought, and those who thought differently were just fooling themselves. Kirsten knew she was more realistic than to ever believe in true love, in happily ever after. Until Allie, that is.

Kirsten had been dating first one woman then another when she came across Allison Sullivan and decided to give her a go. What Kirsten hadn't planned on was the way Allie made her feel. Allie looked up to her, made her know she was special and wanted. Slowly, she found herself falling for Allie. It was just as she was stopping her extracurricular activities that Allie broke it off. Allie wouldn't understand what Kirsten felt, not that Kirsten could've even explained it to her — how things just don't last, how you've got to watch out for yourself because nobody else will. Allie wouldn't even believe it when Kirsten said there were no other women anymore.

When Allie left the room that day, after Kirsten offered her a second chance, Kirsten knew what she had to do. She had to make sure Allie would miss her, that Allie would find no one else and would be alone. It was pure genius that she got Allie's new girlfriend Tina in bed with her, and that Allie caught them. That day she knew she had won round one.

Kirsten moved to the quick bebop rhythm of Erasure and smiled at her dance partner, Cybill. Earlier in the night Kirsten had danced by herself on one of Backstreet's elevated dancing platforms but decided Cybill was just too cute to pass up.

Kirsten still loved Allie and didn't care what she had to do, or whom she had to sleep with, to prove to Allie that she was the only one for her. The only one who would be faithful, the only one who would love her like she deserved to be loved.

Cybill followed Kirsten off the dance floor and stopped a waitress to order a beer for herself and a soda for Kirsten.

"Sure you don't want something a bit stronger?" Cybill asked, indicating Kirsten's soda.

"I'm sure," Kirsten replied. "You know, I just can't shake the feeling that I know you from somewhere."

"In a community this small, chances are you do," Cybill replied, laughing, clearly enjoying Kirsten's attention.

Kirsten sipped her soda, letting the cool liquid stream down her dry throat. A friend of Cybill's came over and the two chatted for a few moments. Kirsten just wished she could remember where she knew Cybill from.

Just then she caught a snippet of what Cybill's friend was saying to her: ". . . yeah, and then that friend of yours . . ."

"Allie?" Cybill asked.

"Yeah, her. Then she left with the woman from the House of Kinsey . . ."

"Brett Higgins? The manager?"

Kirsten suddenly realized where she had seen Cybill before: in pictures on Allie's dresser! The two had been best friends for several years, and Kirsten always thought Allie harbored more than mere friendship for Cybill. Kirsten suddenly knew what she must do to ensure that Allie didn't forget about her.

"Wanna dance?" Kirsten seductively asked Cybill, but even as Cybill followed her to the dance floor, she began thinking that she should visit the House of Kinsey in the next day or two. She wanted to cover all the bases possible. But first she'd have Allie's best friend.

Later that night as they left to go to Cybill's apartment, driving through the cold winter air to continue their dance under the covers with only the beat of their hearts to guide their wild gyrations, Kirsten had etched into her memory one name: Brett.

CHAPTER 5
Meetings

Allie drove to Warren, carefully following the directions Brett had given her up to the newly completed I-696 and across to Mound, wondering if she was really doing the right thing.

She had noticed the woman glancing at her throughout the meeting, and as she sized Brett up, the thought occurred to her that she may be just what she was looking for. There was something different about her, very different from Tina or Kirsten or anyone else she had been with. Something dark and mysterious and driven. She had been afraid Brett would leave when she went to the restroom and was relieved to find her still there, although Shelly had immediately pounced on her.

She didn't know yet if she was in over her head or what — she just knew she couldn't back down now. Allie had only dated women her own age or slightly older, and she guessed Brett to be at least 25, older than any of them. But she grinned as she remembered the flustered look on Brett's face when she whispered the come-on in her ear.

Brett got home and turned on just enough lights to create a mood. She locked the briefcase in her closet safe, hung up her jacket and then selected a Marvin Gaye CD, which she turned on low.

Her home was a modest two-story bungalow decorated in earth tones and wood grains. A breezeway in the front led to the living room, which had a library off to the side. These rooms were completely carpeted in a deep blue. The stereo, TV and VCR were housed in an oak entertainment center, facing a couch on the opposing wall. The kitchen, with its parquet floor, was just beyond, and the bedroom, bathroom and laundry room were in the back, adjacent to a sunroom and a covered back porch. The entire upstairs was devoted to Brett's office.

The garage was unattached, one of the few things Brett disliked about the place, and was further back in the yard.

Brett had grown up in a disorganized house and

vowed to never allow her place to fall into such a state. Magazines were always put away in the proper place in the library, dishes always washed and CDs replaced as soon as she finished listening to them. Fortunately, since she spent very little time at home and rarely cooked for herself, there wasn't much to keeping up her vow.

She went to the bathroom to brush her teeth before Allie arrived. She paused for a moment in front of the full-length mirror. Her black jeans were just tight enough to accentuate her ass and muscular thighs. She had already pulled the wallet out of her back pocket and carefully rolled the sleeves on her black T-shirt to show off her arms, then adjusted the black leather, studded cock ring she wore on her wrist. She thought there was a certain irony to a lesbian wearing a C-ring on her wrist, even though most people thought it was merely a nifty bracelet. Besides that, the only jewelry she wore was an Ironman watch, her college class ring and a gold necklace.

Her thick, slightly wavy black hair was lying just right tonight, but she ran her hands through it anyway, ensuring the way it fell behind her ears and left her with small sideburns.

She shut off the bathroom light and went down the hall to the living room. Just then the doorbell rang.

Brett stopped briefly before opening the door to catch her thoughts and realized she was nervous. She had become accustomed to dealing with people in the adult industry, where talk was free and sex was easy. She wasn't used to dealing with women far removed from that atmosphere, and everything about Allie said that she was a young, middle-class white girl from the right side of the tracks.

As soon as she opened the door, Brett thought, "Wow." The streetlights glistened off the snow that lay lightly on the ground, creating a dazzling effect around Allie with her blond hair and brown jacket.

Allie shivered and Brett quickly ushered her through the entry and into the living room. "Welcome to my humble abode," she said, taking Allie's jacket.

"Nice place."

"It's not much — I'm not really into decorating. I prefer things to be functional, livable and comfortable."

Allie gestured to a couple of barbells on the floor. "You work out?"

"Yeah, I have a full bench and set-up in the basement."

"Looks good on you." Allie slowly looked Brett over.

"Thanks."

Allie began to look at the framed posters on the walls.

"That's a Keith Haring," Brett said.

"It's cool."

"Yeah — sometimes it makes me think of something a kid would do. It's simple and cuts right to the heart of the matter." Brett had actually bought it for Quinn's birthday a few years back, but Quinn had caught Brett cheating on her and dumped her. So Brett kept the print for herself.

Allie turned and Brett became immediately conscious that they were mere inches from each other. As they looked directly into each other's eyes, Brett inhaled Allie's perfume, a provocative womanly musk. She leaned a bit closer, but something in Allie's eyes made her pull back.

"And over there," Brett said, easing the tension in the room, if not in herself, "is one of my favorites." She pointed out her "Because" poster. It said simply, "Because," listing about a hundred things and closed with "I am a part of the lesbian/gay civil rights movement."

Brett watched Allie as she read the poster. Her hair fell gracefully over her shoulders and down her back, and her long eyelashes flashed as she read the poster's small type, her slender body unconsciously leaning toward the poster. As if she felt Brett's gaze upon her, she turned and smiled. Brett wasn't used to being almost eye-to-eye with another woman.

"Can I get you anything to drink?" Brett asked, ashamed at having been caught staring.

"Coke."

"Don't wanna risk my getting you drunk and taking advantage of you, huh?"

Allie shrugged nervously, so Brett left to get a Coke for Allie and a Miller Lite for herself. When she returned a few moments later, Allie was sitting on the couch. Brett handed her the soda and sat next to her.

"That's so right," Allie said, indicating the poster.

"Yeah, I was a real little activist in college and that poster was my battle cry," she said, looking into the clear blue of Allie's eyes.

"Doesn't it sometimes seem that nothing'll make any difference?"

"If you believe that, you might as well kill yourself right now. I myself firmly believe that everyone can make a difference, if only to a handful of people."

"Are you from around here?"

"I grew up in Detroit . . ."

"Oh, really, where?"

"East side," Brett replied. Anything east of Woodward was considered the east side of Detroit. "I went to Pershing High School. I bought this house after I graduated from college."

"You own it?"

"Yeah, it means a mortgage and all, but I'm ahead in my payments. I've got a decent job."

"Doin' what?"

"A little of this and a lot of that, and yourself?" She didn't want to tell Allie what she did for a living. At least, not yet.

"Well, I've got a job," Allie said shyly, "but I still live with my parents up near Seventeen and Ryan."

"Ah, Sterile Whites," Brett replied, quoting the oft-used nickname of the bedroom community.

"Like Warren is much different."

"Yeah," Brett said with one of her most endearing grins. "We're blue-collar, you're white collar."

"So you're saying you fit in here — what do you do for a living? Work at GM?"

"Nah, I just meant that it's too . . . um . . . sterile up there for me. Down here I'm a bit closer to the city. But if I had known the area better when I bought this place, I probably would've got a place in Royal Oak or Ferndale . . ."

"Yeah, I can see you fitting in there," Allie replied with a grin.

"So, do you go to school?"

"Yeah, in Sterling Heights."

"I didn't know they had a college there." They were sitting next to each other on the couch. She put her arm on the back of the couch behind Allie.

"I'm still in high school."

"Oh." She knew Allie was young, but not that young.

"I plan on starting college next year," Allie explained.

"So you're a senior." Brett pushed her hand back through her hair. She didn't want to be accused of recruiting minors. She didn't think it was right when she saw older people going after teenagers. They should offer these kids support and advice, not use them as sex toys. She pulled her arm back into her own lap.

"Yeah. I graduate in seven months." Allie watched her closely, as if gauging the variety of emotions that passed over Brett's face and balancing them with what she heard in Brett's voice and how Brett looked in those black jeans.

"So what do you want to study in college?"

"Criminal Justice."

"Ah, but do you really believe there's any true justice left in the world?"

"I guess I'm kinda like you with gay rights, that I have to believe that I can make a difference." Allie moved a bit closer to her.

"If justice is blind, she must be a blind whore — bought and sold by the highest bidder. We are privileged to live in a country that will kill people based on their skin color, while the guilty are allowed to walk free as long as they have enough power and money."

"There is no easy solution, but I promise my justice will be dispensed equally."

Brett laughed and they looked into each other's eyes.

"Cat's eyes," Allie said suddenly.

"What?" Brett pulled herself out of the blue pools of Allie's eyes, where she had found herself momentarily lost.

"You've got cat's eyes."

"I guess so — depends on what's happening." She was enjoying this conversation. She took another sip of her beer. "They vary from hazel to brown to green, depending on the mood I'm in."

"So what does it mean when they're green?" Allie asked coyly.

"That's for me to know, and you to find out." Brett ran a finger along Allie's jaw. Allie grabbed Brett's hand and kissed it.

"I think I'll enjoy solving that mystery."

"I've gotta ask, just how old are you?"

Allie hesitated. "Seventeen."

Seventeen was young, Brett thought, and she didn't want to be this girl's first lesbian lover, let alone deal with the possibility that Allie was still a virgin . . .

Allie reached over and put her deliciously long-fingered hand along the line of Brett's jaw, turned Brett toward her and kissed her full on the lips.

Brett responded tentatively at first, enjoying Allie's lips and mouth. She pulled Allie closer, and they twisted and turned, making out on the couch. Brett knew she could have Allie, but told herself she had to be careful with Allie, because of her age, but really there was something more to it. Something that came up when she looked into Allie's eyes.

An hour and a half later they were still fully clothed on the couch when Brett looked at her watch and realized she had to leave.

"Where do you have to go this late at night?" Allie stood and readjusted her clothing.

"Oh, just the usual — run some arms down to Mexico and exchange them for drugs." Brett pushed her hand back through her hair.

They traded phone numbers, and slowly kissed good-bye. Brett slid her hands over Allie's tight ass, but Allie pulled away.

"Don't you have somewhere to go?"

When Allie pulled into the driveway, the porch-light was on. She glanced at her watch, 12:30. Her curfew was 11 p.m. on school nights. Her father was sitting in the living room reading *Clear and Present Danger.* He looked up, took off his glasses, put the end of the earpiece into his mouth, glanced at his watch and smiled.

"C'mere, kitten," he said, taking his feet off the footrest and patting it. For as long as Allie could remember, John Sullivan had had thick white hair that rode his head in waves. It gave him a dignified, wise look.

She sat on the recliner's matching, padded footrest and stared at the ground, knowing she was late and deserved whatever lecture he gave. He reached over and raised her head to look into her eyes. Some people said she had his eyes, but she could only hope to ever have the love that shone through in his. Although she loved both her parents dearly, she knew she had to love them while she had them, for they were already in their sixties and she worried about them.

"Are you going to tell me what's going on?" he asked.

"What do you mean?"

"You've been acting differently lately. You never had a problem making your curfew before."

"I'm sorry, I won't let it happen again."

He stared at her while she turned away, then he leaned back in the recliner. "Is there some boy you don't want meeting your crotchety old man?"

"Dad!"

"C'mon now, kitten, I know there must be some reason you've suddenly started acting differently — not telling us where you're going, who you're with . . ." He let his sentence trail off. "Allie, I know your Mom and I aren't exactly hip and with it, but I do know I've got an attractive daughter and that someday she's gonna bring home some boy to meet us."

"Dad, there's no boy I want to bring home to meet you." She got up, turned away from him and began to finger the crystal figurines in the armoire.

"Something's going on, and I'd like to think that I can help. You're my daughter, you know, and I'll love you no matter what."

That last phrase did it. She knew she had to do

this but was afraid to. She had heard so many horror stories during youth group that no matter how much she believed her parents would be different, it still chilled her to the bones, but she couldn't go on lying to them. She leaned against the wall and a tear slid down her cheek.

"Oh, Allison, whatever it is, it can't be that bad," he said, coming over and pulling her toward him.

"Daddy," she said, wrapping her arms around him. He held her until her spasms subsided and she leaned back against the armoire. She pulled herself up to her full height and took a deep breath. "Dad." She looked down at the ground. He raised her chin to look into her eyes. "There's something I've wanted to tell you . . ."

"What?" he gently urged.

"I won't be bringing any guys home to meet you." She went to the front window, where she stood with her arms crossed and gazed outside. She had started this, it had to be done, she couldn't go on lying and she couldn't chicken out. She turned to face him, suddenly realizing how old he was. "Daddy, I won't be bringing any guys home to meet you because I'm gay." There, she said it, it was out now. And so was she.

A sudden deer-in-the-headlights look crossed his face. She could feel her heart beating in her chest, feel her face turn red with fear. "You're kidding me, right?" he finally said.

She shook her head. She took a step toward him, not liking to see the pain in his eyes. "Dad, I'd like to apologize to you for this, but I can't. It's too much a part of who I am."

"Allie . . ." He took a hesitant step toward her,

then shook his head. "I'm sorry." He looked away, then began toying with his glasses. He put them back on and turned toward her. "Are you sure?"

"Yes, Daddy. I'm sure. Very sure."

"So much is going through my mind right now. I want to know why, and how you're so sure." He gave a half-hearted smile. "But then I don't think I want to know." They stood looking at each other, and Allie stood straight, not allowing herself to flinch under his gaze. "Kitten," he finally said, "I just know you're my daughter and I love you no matter what." A tear rolled down his cheek and Allie stepped forward so they could wrap their arms around each other.

Brett glanced at her watch as she pulled up in McDonald's dark parking lot. 11:58. She parked next to the Thunderbird, checked the heavy sureness of the .357 against her breast, climbed out, pulled the briefcase out of the trunk and set the car alarm.

She pulled another set of keys out of her pocket and unlocked the old Thunderbird. As she pulled out of the parking lot, she carefully looked around to make sure no one was watching her before she headed into Detroit.

The light snow covering the ground only accented the darkness as she headed south on Hoover to Eight Mile, which she'd take across to Woodward. The streetlights cast strange shadows as they caught the lightly falling flakes. She flipped through the radio stations until she found her favorite all-70s station, Star 97 FM.

Brett cursed the falling snow; it always made

driving more difficult. Especially high-speed driving. But there shouldn't be a need for that tonight. Regardless, she reminded herself of the Michigander's creed: "Don't like the weather? Wait fifteen minutes and it'll change."

There are certain areas of Detroit that don't need the cover solace of darkness in order to be foreboding. They were shrouded with danger even when enveloped with the sweltering heat and sunshine of summer. Even when the grass, such as it was, was green, and a warm breeze blew through your hair, you could still see the broken flickering of neon signs, feel the crags and holes of the ill-repaired streets under your tires, smell the smoke from the nearest factory or last house burning, hear the sirens and distant shots and screams carried faintly on the breeze. The city had a way of attacking all of the senses. Perhaps, Brett thought, it was nature's way of telling people who didn't belong there to run the hell out as quickly as possible. Unless, of course, the city was home, in which case you became immune to the cacophony.

Although she lived in Warren, and had lived across the state when she went to school, her real home was Detroit. Not only had she grown up and gone to school there, but all her work was now centered there. She knew the area, the attitudes and the cops. While a lot of young white women avoided Detroit unless they worked there, she felt most comfortable there. In the suburbs, people cared too much about what the other guy was doing.

As she drove, carefully avoiding as many potholes as possible, Brett noticed how many of the streetlights were burnt out. At this time of night, not too many people were outside — only a few who lived on the streets. Brett enjoyed the quiet of the almost dark streets and the gloom that covered this desolate part of the city at night. She enjoyed its solace, its danger.

She saw the unlit Palmer Park off to the right and pulled down the street to the parking lot. During the summer, people would be here until quite late — but not this late. And definitely not when the brutal winter winds began to beat the city.

A small access road labeled "No Motor Vehicles" was blocked by a parked car, which she assumed to be Ralph's. She searched for anything out of the ordinary, anything to be wary of. When she saw nothing, she parked the car a few feet from Ralph's, moved her gun into her pocket, pulled her scarf and jacket tighter about her and grabbed the briefcase. As she walked across the barren park to the access road and followed that up to the restrooms, she wished she had worn boots and her warmer trenchcoat. There wasn't supposed to be this much snow tonight.

The building that housed the restrooms was amazingly large for its purpose. It had obviously been built during Detroit's heyday — even its graceful architecture reflected a certain grandeur compared to its surroundings. Complete with chimney, it looked like a graceful brick house from decades ago.

"If only Mom could see me now," Brett muttered under her breath, her words freezing in the air.

She rounded the corner of the far side of the building and a man stepped out of the arched doorway to the men's room. He was dressed all in black with a scarf tied around the bottom half of his face.

Ralph watched far too many spy movies for his own good.

"You got the cash?" he said when she was still a few feet away. Brett waved the briefcase and nodded.

"Lemme see it."

"Lemme see the goods first," she replied. His voice sounded different. Probably just the cold, or the scarf. She hoped. Just then she felt something in the center of her back. And it wasn't a crick.

"Just hand the dough over." The man in front of her stepped out from the shadow of the building and pulled his scarf down. It wasn't Ralph. She sized him up: rather short, muscular and uglier than a tree frog. Something about him read that he was just someone's gofer, which of course she herself sometimes was, but she was exceptional in that her IQ was greater than the number of rings she wore on her fingers.

She played shy. She played naïve. She played blond bombshell, which was difficult, given her black hair.

"What, what's going on?" she said in her best little-girl voice.

"Oh, Jesus — this has got to be a joke," said a deep voice from behind her. She felt the gun at her back being lowered.

"I . . . I was just supposed to switch cases . . ."

"Leo! You gotta be kiddin' me — I can't believe this shit, that wimp Rick DeSilva's sendin' a little girl to do a guy's job!" the man behind her said, stepping away from her. She noticed he was taller and stockier than Leo, his skin so black it barely reflected the moonlight.

"She's s'posed to be his top man, Johnny," Leo said.

"Who's Rick?" she said.

"Je-sus!" Leo said, laughing. "This is just too god-damned funny!"

"I say we really take care of her." Johnny pocketed his gun and reached for his zipper. "Real good care of her."

She figured it'd take them a few seconds to get their guns out and this was the best chance she'd have. As she pulled her gun, Leo noticed the quick movement and started to pull his. She got off one shot at Johnny before Leo had his gun out. She dove for the ground and rolled, still clutching the briefcase. His first shot missed her by a mile.

"Get her!" Leo yelled, running after her as Johnny cursed and hopped about. She had clipped his thigh. Fortunately, her car wasn't very far away, but it was locked. And for once in her life, Brett thanked God for the snow, because Leo hit an icy patch as he fired again, totally missing her. But Johnny had his gun out and was firing. Brett dove, hitting the pavement of the access road.

"Get the car — I'll get her!" Leo yelled, hot in pursuit. Brett came up from her dive, hurdled the railing to cut across the grass and fired at the passenger's window of her car, smashing the glass. She zigged and zagged, avoiding the bullets, then threw the briefcase through the shattered window and dove in after it. Leo was there when she revved the engine and headed onto the street — the curb here was too high for her to haul across the lawn without risking her car.

They were right behind her as she screeched

down the road. She heard a gunshot and the back window shattered. She turned onto McNichols while Leo reloaded and began shooting out the passenger's window. She threw a U-turn across a median and headed for the freeway. They spun out slightly getting around the turn but were right on her tail in a few seconds. She tried firing out the driver's window a few times, hitting their windshield, but then she almost slipped into a telephone pole when she hit a pothole. She ran the lights and counted on the fact she could outrun them on the highway, and if that didn't work, that she knew the area better than they did.

She hit the freeway, heading south, and went flying toward the East Davison on-ramp, but another car pulled on ahead of her. She cursed and looked to turn off, but the concrete walls on both sides prevented that. She took a breath and floored it, flying past the car on the narrow shoulder, briefly slamming into the wall.

Leo and Johnny struck the other car full speed, sending it careening against the wall. Brett soared onto the freeway. She gunned it and raced toward the finish where the freeway ended.

She headed south into Hamtramck. She shot through the side streets and constantly checked her mirrors for any sign of the blue sedan. Seeing none, she felt a little relief. Nonetheless, she wound her way through the streets, ensuring they would not find her.

As she tried to cool her adrenaline rush and recenter herself, she drove through the streets, silently promising herself to spend more time at the shooting range. She barely noticed the old houses and the names of the funeral parlors around her — Dzielinski, Lewandowski, Jerzewski. Hamtramck was Detroit's own Little Poland, surrounded on all sides by the city, but still standing with its own individuality, with *paczkis* on Fat Tuesday and Catholic churches and centers on every other corner. In her youth she had admired the place, now she noticed the cars on blocks in the streets, the lack of lighting and the disrepair the grand old homes were falling into.

It was just as she was thinking of the old joke about the reason all Polish names end with "-ski" (because they couldn't spell "toboggan"), and considering the similar number of churches in her own Catholic Polish and Italian eastside neighborhood that she felt a vibration in her pants pocket. She pulled out her pager and swore when she saw the number to the Paradise Theater. She looked around and didn't see the sedan, so she began searching for a working pay phone. If she was in her own car, she'd have her cell phone handy, but not in this beat-up old crate. On the third try, she found one that worked.

"Paradise Theater . . ." Ted slurred into the phone.

Great, she thought. He's drunk again. "Yeah, Ted, this is Brett . . ."

"Brett! Storm's in the office . . . Some guys charged the stage . . ."

"Put her on."

Storm's voice was shaky, she was trying not to cry. "Brett?" she said hopefully.

Brett's heart twitched a little. "What's the matter?"

"There were some guys, and . . ." She started to cry again.

"I'll be there in ten to twenty."

"Thank you."

"You're very welcome."

"And Brett?" Storm said, tentatively.

"Yes, dear?"

"Um, nothing. 'Bye." With that the phone went dead.

Brett turned the heat in the car up to high, lit a cigarette and drove with her jacket wrapped tightly around her. With the adrenaline leaving her body, she suddenly felt a pain in her thigh. She lowered her hand to feel it, and brought the hand back up, covered in blood. Damn it, even though she shot and shattered the window, it must've still got her.

Storm. She had given the girl that stage name shortly after she hired her. Her real name was Pamela, but from the first moment Brett knew she was a storm of anger and emotions and fear. Brett had seen hundreds of women come and go at the Paradise — some lasted only a few weeks, others clung on for as long as they could, but Brett's job was to make the theater money. She kept girls on only as long as the men wanted to see them, although the incredible diversity of her clientele welcomed a like configuration of dancers: black, white, tall, short, big breasts and slender frames.

The dancers rotated. If booked, they would only work one week, or weekend, per month. But they could, if they wanted to, make enough cash in that short period of time to survive for the rest of the month.

When Storm first came in looking for a job, Brett knew right from the start that she was underage. But she was good-looking, sensual and clean, with long black hair that rode over her shoulders in thick waves, olive skin that appeared tanned in the middle of winter and the shapely curves of a more mature woman. Brett knew if she handled Storm right, she would make them both a lot of money, which she did.

But those were all excuses, really. The reason Brett, who was dead set against any form of child pornography, took a chance with Storm was because of what she knew about the girl and the world. From the first, Brett knew much more about Storm than Storm ever wanted to admit, but that was only because Brett had once been there herself. Not exactly, but close enough to know.

Storm's stepfather repeatedly raped her from the time she was nine years old. Her mother refused to believe anything Storm said when she finally got up the courage to tell. Storm repeatedly ran away from home and was repeatedly brought back until, one day, when she was sixteen, she ran so fast, so far, she ended up in Michigan. When she got to Detroit from Gary, Indiana, she had no money, no home and no job. She couldn't take a job that might give her parents any indication where she was, so she applied to the Paradise for a job as a dancer.

Brett knew the only other option Storm had was to be a prostitute, and she liked the girl. She created phony papers for her, helped her get her GED and find a place to live. Her abusive stepfather had beaten her so low that she had no self-esteem, so she never had a problem selling herself to the men — but only as a dancer, unlike many of the others who worked as prostitutes on the side to help support their drug habits.

Brett saw a reflection of herself every time she

looked at Storm. She knew that if Storm was ever going to find her self-respect, she was going to have to do it on her own. Brett could help, but she couldn't do it for her. In Storm's eyes she saw the purity, innocence and naiveté that resided in the curvaceous, sexy body of the woman who was now eighteen years old.

Brett threw the cigarette out the window and pulled into the parking lot. She reloaded and chambered her gun before grabbing the briefcase and, with her hand on the gun in her pocket, she headed into the Paradise Theater.

CHAPTER 6
In the Chill of the Night

Inside the box office, which was lit only by the TV, Storm was huddled on a simple wooden chair in the far corner. She looked up at Brett with the eyes of a scared little girl. Ted was sitting at the desk with his feet propped up and his chair leaned back. He was watching an old rerun of *The Love Boat*.

"Hey, Brett." His breath reeked of alcohol and his

eyes were dazed. "Our girl over here has had a tough night . . ."'

"Leave us alone."

"Okay." He walked out the door to the gay side.

Brett went to Storm, who gazed at the floor. Brett knelt in front of her and gently lifted Storm's chin so their eyes met.

Storm's eyes were filled with questions Brett could never answer, and a tear slowly slid down her cheek. Brett caught it with her thumb, took one of Storm's hands and slowly brought it up to her lips and kissed it, then pulled Storm into her arms.

"Hey! The movie's out over here!" Ted yelled through the bullet-proof glass.

"Well, get your ass in here and fix it!" Brett looked at Storm. "You ready to blow this pop stand?"

Storm nodded. Brett went upstairs and locked the briefcase in Rick's wall safe. She came back down, put her arm around Storm and they went to the dressing room to gather Storm's belongings before heading out to the car.

"Isn't it a little cold to have the window down?" Storm asked at the car.

"It's not down, it's gone," Brett said, tossing Storm's stuff into the back seat and opening the door for her.

Storm looked her up and down before climbing into the car. "You've had a tough night. Thank you for coming to get me." She wrapped her arms around Brett's neck and buried her face in her collar.

"Everything's gonna be all right."

Brett brushed the broken glass from the seat

before they got in. They traveled in cold silence. Brett put her arm around Storm to try to keep her warm. Many people mistook Brett for a man, but Storm never had. She had known right from the start what Brett was, and she liked it.

Since that first night, Brett had been Storm's guardian angel — watching over her, protecting her and comforting her. She was also Storm's sometimes lover. Since that night, Storm was guaranteed a week's booking a month at the Paradise and most men had learned not to abuse her, if not treat her with respect. More than one had felt the metal of Brett's brass knuckles or the steel of her pistol butt. Anyone who abused Storm had the wrath of Brett to face, with Rick's full blessings. Not only did Rick like to see the violent, primal side of Brett, he also liked to see street scum put in their place. And it didn't hurt that Storm brought the men in like maggots to rotting flesh. Ticket sales soared as the johns flocked to see her dance.

Sometimes Storm dreamed of more, but she also knew how much better off she was now than she had been. Brett didn't know she had played the dangerous game of hooking on the streets of Detroit, and she never would. Even now Storm was offered large amounts of money to prostitute herself, but she would never do that again, if only because she wouldn't be able to look into Brett's face ever again.

Storm only allowed herself to dream of the realistic — like the day she would graduate from college. She had only recently gotten her GED, but she was already taking classes at Wayne State University. She dreamed of her graduation and the look she would find in Brett's eyes on that day.

Storm turned and studied Brett's profile, her black hair, the solemn set of her jaw, the stern mouth. Storm's gaze traveled to the grace of Brett's hands on the steering wheel before returning to Brett's face. At a red light, Brett turned to see Storm looking at her, smiled and took Storm's hand.

"I haven't seen anyone following us, so we're safe," Brett assured her, squeezing her hand.

"Your reputation is becoming known."

Brett grinned at that and kept driving toward Storm's house in Highland Park.

Once there, Brett grabbed the clothes from the backseat and walked Storm up the dark path. Only two streetlights worked in this neighborhood, where enormous houses stood empty or were occupied by only one or two people. Even though many of the homes were falling apart at the seams, they would still be worth a small fortune if only they were a dozen miles further north along the Woodward corridor, in more livable areas like Royal Oak, or the very elite Bloomfield, with one of the highest per capita incomes in the state.

At the moment, Storm only occupied the lower level of her enormous two-story home which she had almost half paid off. She intended to begin using the second story of it once she had it cleaned and painted. Of course, she could only work on that during her spare time, which she didn't have too much of, so it was likely to be quite a while before that happened.

Storm dug out her key and let herself in. She

turned to Brett, who stood just outside the threshold, and motioned her inside.

She was glad to be home. The old, sparse furnishings, largely gathered from dumpsters and curbsides, sometimes with Brett's help, were cozy and reassuring. She lived alone and treasured her few belongings.

She stood in the middle of the room feeling stranded. The night seemed to wash over her, and she brought her shoulders in and held herself as she turned away from Brett, not liking anyone, especially Brett, to see her like this. But Brett was the only one who could see her like this. She felt Brett's strong arms wrap around her and felt herself being lifted from the ground. Brett sat in an old rocking armchair, holding Storm on her lap. She cuddled in closer.

"So what happened?" Brett asked.

"I was giving someone a lap dance and he tore my g-string off . . ." Her voice faded as she remembered the man's grimy hands, her fear as he pulled out his dick and tried to rape her in a room full of people. Her repulsion at the smell of him. Her knowledge that, once again, no one could help her. That no one was there for her if he brutally took her over and over again.

Brett caressed Storm's shoulder trying to contain her anger, trying to see what Storm was describing, and what she wasn't.

"What happened?" Brett's throat was tight with emotion.

"I screamed and it was still early enough that Ted was conscious, so he put on the lights and got the guard and I escaped during the confusion."

Brett pulled Storm in tighter and ran her hands reassuringly over her arms and hair. She kissed her on the forehead and asked, "What about the guys that rushed the stage?"

"It was the end of the last show . . ." Storm clenched up as if trying to block the memory.

"And?"

"And a coupla guys jumped onstage and pinned me down and said they'd have me one way or the other because they know where I live and no white-ass bitch is gonna tease them like I do and not put out anything." Her last words became choked as she began to cry and shake.

"Hey, hey, it's okay," Brett said, gently rocking her in her arms. "They were just bluffing."

"But they said the neighbor's Doberman doesn't scare them!"

Brett knew Storm had been followed before and, although dead men tell no tales, it could happen again. Brett pulled out her .357, slid open the chamber to ensure that a bullet was there, and put it on the table next to them.

They rocked back and forth in silence, because no words could protect Storm from the darkness of the past and present, and no matter what assurances Brett offered, they would be just words. But Brett wanted her, at least for tonight, to feel safe. Brett pulled a tissue from her pocket and dried Storm's eyes and face, and Storm blew her nose and cuddled with Brett again. Brett moaned and pulled her weight off her injured leg.

"What's the matter?" Storm asked, her face dark with sudden concern.

"Oh, it's nothing," Brett assured her, but Storm could obviously read through Brett's cavalier attitude. She gingerly reached down and felt along Brett's thigh.

"Omigod, Brett, honey, you're hurt." She examined her bloodied hand. "What happened?"

"Nothing much, I think I just caught a chunk of glass."

Storm knew better than to ask questions so she hurried down the hall and returned a few moments later with peroxide, tweezers, gauze, surgical tape, a wet washcloth and a few towels. She was used to taking care of Brett's occasional wounds. "Take your pants off," she instructed.

"Hold on, now, I'm the butch here." Brett paused only momentarily before undoing her belt and dropping her jeans. She lay on the couch while Storm carefully cleaned the cut and pulled the glass out. She focused not on the tweezers pulling the glass out of her leg, but instead on the tender touches Storm applied to her leg and the way her hand occasionally glanced across Brett's inner thigh.

"Okay, honey, this is gonna hurt a bit," Storm warned before dousing the laceration with peroxide.

Nearly two decades before, Brett had taught herself not to scream or show pain. At least now she had the gentle, loving touch of Storm to help her keep that promise.

Several minutes later, after Storm had sealed the wound with butterfly stitches and wrapped an ace bandage around Brett's leg, Brett turned and took her into her arms, resuming their former position on the chair. Storm snuggled into Brett, obviously feeling secure despite Brett's injured leg.

A while later, Storm reluctantly pulled away from the safety of Brett's arms. "I'd better take a shower or you'll never get the smell out of your clothes."

Brett nodded, and Storm left the room to jump into a hot shower, no doubt to try to scrub the feel of the men's hands off of her.

Brett glanced about the room one more time, got up, poured herself a drink from the bottle of Glenfiddich Storm kept for her, and walked into the bathroom. She parted the shower curtain. Storm turned to face her, in shock, gasped and covered her breasts with the washcloth. Reluctantly, she let Brett move her hands away from her breasts, and Brett stood holding Storm's hands as she eyed Storm's naked body. Brett guessed she felt her nakedness more than she ever did onstage.

Brett brought her lips to Storm's and they kissed as the water from the shower came down on them like a thunderstorm's rain.

"You're gonna get wet," Storm panted, pulling back.

"Do I look like I care?" Brett pulled Storm's mouth back to her own.

Brett grabbed a towel and left the bathroom silently. She dried her hair as she wandered through the small house and looked at Storm's books and knickknacks. She was holding a picture of Storm with her real parents when Storm entered wearing only a filmy red negligee. Her nipples pressed up against the thin fabric.

Brett smiled. "You're beautiful."

Storm blushed and turned away, but Brett caught

her chin in her hand and brought her face back to her. Wordlessly, Brett picked her up and carried her to the bedroom. Brett pulled off her blazer before climbing on top of her. She kissed her forehead, smelled her hair, ran her tongue along the edge of Storm's ear.

"I want you."

"You know I'm yours."

They looked into each other's eyes, and Brett remembered the first time she saw Storm dance. She'd come back after the show with a dozen roses.

Brett kissed her hard, and Storm returned the kiss, clearly taking what she could, taking what she longed for. Brett's tongue searched her mouth, and Brett felt every curve of Storm's body pressed against hers.

Brett moved her thigh between Storm's legs, and Storm arched up against her. She slipped off Storm's negligee and then Storm pushed her onto her back.

Storm undressed Brett with the skill of the practiced, not with the eagerness of discovery, but with passion unleashed, with the heat of need.

Brett lay quivering in anticipation as Storm took off her shirt and ran her tongue over Brett's breasts. She undid her pants with her teeth and pulled them off, ran her tongue over Brett's stomach, legs and up her inner thighs. Brett moaned with growing passion, with growing need . . .

And the two naked bodies flailed in the night, legs, breasts, stomachs, thighs — all was confusion as the two women strained against each other.

Brett gently turned Storm onto her back and moved her hand between Storm's legs, inserting first one, then two, then three fingers.

Storm moaned as Brett worked her tongue down Storm's long body, all the while working her fingers in that wonderful wetness as she tasted the sweet sweat of Storm.

Between Storm's legs, Brett slowly teased her tongue about the outer lips, pressing her chin down, until she finally let herself go and ran her tongue across Storm's clitoris. Storm arched as Brett ran her tongue up and down her clit, as Brett tasted her, lapping up the juices like a kitten at a bowl of milk.

In the waiting stillness of the night, Brett teased Storm's clit as she turned her arm and formed a fist, and then Brett's entire hand was engulfed within Storm and Storm gasped in pleasure.

With Storm on her back, her legs stretched wide open, Brett clenched and unclenched and twisted and turned her fist within the writhing woman beneath her.

It was an act of total intimacy, this complete penetration, and Brett could feel Storm give herself totally to her. Her own heart quickened as she broke out in a sweat of excitement.

Suddenly the silent night was ripped apart by Storm's screams of ecstasy as she came. They lay still, breathing deeply, as Brett licked the remaining wetness, enjoying the taste and perfumed musk. She slowly removed her hand and held the panting Storm tightly in her arms.

After a while, Brett braced herself up on her arms and examined Storm's face, and Storm let herself be examined, and as they looked into each other's eyes in the waning waves of passion, Storm said, "I love you."

Brett looked deep into Storm's eyes, wanting to

say the same in return, but unable to. She just held Storm close until they fell asleep.

Brett woke with a start. She inventoried her senses and realized it was the barking of the next-door neighbor's Doberman that had awakened her. She cursed the mutt, nuzzled her face in Storm's silky hair and started to fall back asleep with her body wrapped around Storm's.

Why was the dog barking at — she looked at the clock — 3 a.m.?

On full alert, she slipped quietly out of bed. As she was putting on her shirt, Storm rolled over. "What's the matter?"

Brett leaned forward and kissed her on the lips. "Just checking out the house."

"Why?"

Just then they heard glass break. Someone was coming through the back door. Storm stared at Brett, her eyes wide in fear.

Brett grabbed for her gun, which she always put on the bedside table, and swore as she realized she had left it in the living room. She glanced around the room for something to use and decided on the bedside lamp, which she quickly unplugged and removed its shade.

"Get dressed, stay here and be quiet," Brett whispered before she left, closing the door behind her.

There was no telling where they might be, Brett thought as she slinked down the hallway, listening. But she had the element of surprise, as well as knowledge of the surroundings.

But they probably had guns. It sounded like there were two of them. She heard a clatter in the kitchen and a whispered "Sshh!" They had taken several minutes getting through the door and, by the noise they made, they were either drunk or drugged. Either way, there was no telling what they would do.

She stood with the lamp at the foot of the hallway, scanning the dark room. She saw a single shadow leave the kitchen and slowly feel its way toward her. Brett silently pushed her arm behind the tall bookcase at the foot of the hallway and waited as the figure blindly approached her. She silently prayed there weren't too many books to weigh down the case as he came closer and closer until . . .

NOW!

He turned as he heard the movement, but his gun went flying as he was hit first with books and then with the bookcase. He yowled, the pain of his broken arm and ribs evidently cutting through his drug-induced stupor as Brett dove for his gun and rolled into the living room.

"What the hell!" his partner yelled, running into the room.

"Watch out!" screamed his buddy.

The standing man was briefly outlined by the light from the front window as he dove, but Brett took aim and fired. She hit his shoulder and sent him sprawling. She jumped to her feet and fired one, then two bullets directly into his head.

"No! Please God, no!" the other man screamed as Brett stepped over and aimed at his head.

"Then shut the fuck up." She kicked his broken ribs, getting even. "Son-of-a-bitch." She brought her hand down fiercely across his face. How could they do this to her? "Scum!" She belted him with the pistol. Never again. Never, ever again.

"Brett?" Storm said quietly from the hall.

Brett took a deep breath, returned to the present and stood. "Page Frankie."

Storm obeyed.

As Brett surveyed the scene, she was shaken. As she had flown through the air after dumping the bookcase, she remembered taking dives like that before, when she was younger and her father had gotten home in a bad mood. In those days, it was all Brett could do to avoid being hit by a flying table, knife or fist. Now, each day, when she worked out, when she lifted hundreds of pounds of steel, when she ran mile after mile, her mantra was "Never again." Never again would she be so defenseless against an attacker. Never again would she be unable to defend herself. Never again would she be beaten and raped. Never again.

Frankie was there twenty minutes later. Barely a word was spoken. He efficiently bound and gagged the unconscious man and bundled up the corpse. Together, she and Frankie hauled them into the trunk of his car.

"That was them," Storm said simply.

Brett kissed her, told her to lock all the doors and not open them for anyone else.

"Cass or the river?" Frankie asked as she climbed into his car.

"Cass." Brett knew these were not bodies they would need to keep secret. The Detroit River would wash the bodies away, conceal them for months or years or, in the case of Jimmy Hoffa, forever, whereas the Cass Corridor would relinquish its bodies much sooner — either when someone who would actually report them to the police tripped over them or smelled the rotting flesh.

No one would be able to connect rett and Frankie with these bodies, or even develop a motive for the murder. And there certainly would not be any repercussions, which there would be if they had offed the leader of another organization.

Frankie drove south on Woodward, within the speed limits, carefully maneuvering on the increasingly slick roads. It had stopped snowing but the temperature had dropped, making the roads into a skating rink. They really didn't need to be pulled over. No further conversation was necessary. Not only did Frankie know better than to ask questions, but he had also seen Storm and Brett and the condition of the house. He knew what had happened.

At this time of night, the hookers and hustlers had called it a day and left the streets. Even the street-people had departed, seeking safer, warmer places to cover themselves with newspapers and slip away into the safe haven of sleep or drug-induced slumber for a while. The city loomed in front of them, growing ever clearer with each mile — the Renaissance Center's high tower reaching for the sky like trees in a forest of desolation. The few streetlights that were not burnt out struck the plumes of steam that rose from gratings in the street to create fantasies of a bad horror film.

Frankie cut across Warren Avenue to Cass, where he hung a left and took it south until they found an old warehouse just a few blocks south of Wayne State University. The massive metal structure was obviously abandoned, with graffiti scrawled across its sides and the entry barred only by a rusting old fence secured with a simple chain and padlock.

Brett took Frankie's lockpicks and deftly made quick work of the lock — she wanted to be able to resecure the building once they had made their little deposit into its safekeeping.

Frankie reached into the trunk and heaved the first body onto the cold, hard pavement. He quickly frisked him, grabbing all identification and valuables, before he tossed the corpse nonchalantly over his shoulders and headed into the dark recesses of what would become its mausoleum.

It took both Brett and Frankie to quietly transport the second fellow, now conscious and struggling, into the interior. As they threw him onto the floor near the first one, he rolled and struggled and fought against his bonds, gag and inevitable doom. Brett pulled out his identification and looked at it.

"Daniel McMartin," she read. She rolled him over and searched for any other identification or valuables. When she was done, she handed it all to Frankie and turned away as he pointed his gun.

"Roach Be Gone." Frankie only needed one shot.

As Brett and Frankie went back to the car, resecuring the chain and padlock behind them, the snow started falling again. They stared at each other over the hood and Frankie shook his head.

"Not Storm. Never Storm," Brett said.

Those were the only words that passed between them. They climbed back into the car and he drove her back to Storm's. If he noticed the condition of the T-Bird, he said nothing.

At 5:30 Storm unlocked the door for Brett. Brett

took Storm in her arms and the two women locked up and went back to bed.

Brett was running through a dark house. The walls of the old mansion seemed to loom in on her, contracting with her every step. Out of breath, she ran for her life, but still he gained on her. She could hear his hot breath just steps behind her. She tripped and fell to the hot, hard floor. He was there, she saw him. He was going to kill her, and there was nothing she could do. The walls billowed in on her.

It was her father. She could never run fast or far enough to escape him. He would always follow her. Day or night, he was always with her. She tried to roll out of his reach, and as she whipped out of the roll and onto her feet, she looked again at him, but it wasn't him.

She woke with a scream, bolting upright in bed. Immediately, Storm's arms were around her, and she could hear Storm's tender voice telling her it was okay, there was nothing to be afraid of, but there was. Storm pulled Brett back down onto the bed and curled up behind her, holding her. Images from the dream continued to play through Brett's head.

"It was someone else, it wasn't him," Brett murmured, shaking like a baby.

"Shh, honey, it's okay. He's never going to get you again."

"But it wasn't him," Brett whispered, slowly falling back to sleep unable to shake the feeling that the dark figure wanted more than her life.

CHAPTER 7
Reverberations

At 10 a.m. Rick was at the door to take Brett to get her car. Frankie had taken care of the T-Bird during the night, transporting it somewhere to be repaired.

"What happened last night?" Rick asked as they got into his black Cadillac.

"Methinks Ralph met his maker." Ralph was okay, Brett thought, for a cop, but she didn't waste too many feelings on any of them.

"And?"

"And I've got a bone to pick with two chumps named Leo and Johnny." Brett detailed the events of the night, and Rick stopped her only to ask questions that would help him identify the thugs or their boss. Nothing was said about Storm or about Brett and Frankie's midnight run. "I want them, Rick," Brett said as they reached the McDonald's where she had left her Probe.

"You can have them, because I want their boss."

Rick, Frankie and Brett had grown to know one another so well that few words were usually necessary between them. They could read one another's silences, attitudes and tones so well that one might accuse them of telepathy.

Frankie and Rick had been together for five years, ever since Rick had taken over the business from his father. In his father's day, though, it was much smaller and concerned only with legal, adult goods. Rick decided not to stop there. He was interested in more money, more power and greater notoriety.

Where Brett was Rick's right hand as far as brains went, Frankie was his left when it came to the physical. Frankie wasn't stupid, but he didn't have Brett's knowledge and intuition about business — he understood beating people up, protecting people and killing people. He was the usual choice when it came to situations like Brett's midnight exchange. He was strong, reliable and effective.

Brett didn't need to stop by her home, because she had already showered and changed at Storm's, so she immediately headed for Adult Fantasies, one of the bookstores Rick owned on Eight Mile, to check in on things.

* * * * *

That morning, Allie awoke, bleary-eyed and tired, with a smile on her face. This did not slip by her father, who read the newspaper over breakfast as usual. She wished she could tell what he was thinking, but the only thing unusual she noticed was the somewhat wistful stare she caught him at as she left.

The day at school went pretty much as usual, with Allie sleeping through her first-hour English class and being confused during second-hour science. She decided to skip third-hour computer class, since she hadn't for a while, and she really needed to go to the local convenience store with John and Rich to get a Big Gulp and a candy bar. But during fourth-hour math, Derek Needleman, the captain of the football team, approached her.

"Hey, Sullivan," he said, putting his big, meaty paw on her shoulder.

She yanked away in disgust. "Whaddya want?"

"Was that you I saw down by the Backstage last weekend?"

"Backstage?"

"Yeah, that queer bar in Detroit."

"What were you doin' hangin' around a queer bar?" Allie replied, while several people around her snickered.

"You dyke," he said, grabbing her shoulder again.

"Mr. Needleman," the teacher said, getting Derek's attention. "Would you care to show the class how we solve for a variable on both sides of the equation?"

* * * * *

It only took a few hours for Brett to stop by several of the bookstores — looking at the books, writing the weekly employee schedules and putting together product orders — because quite a few of them were located along Eight Mile.

Along Eight Mile, the south side was a line-up of adult bookstores, titty bars and Arab-owned mom-and-pop convenience stores that proclaimed, "Check Cashing — No ID Required."

She knew she was in for a day, though, when the manager of the first store looked at her and said, "Hey, Brett, the butt plugs are selling like hotcakes!" She still couldn't believe he managed to say that with a straight face.

In fact, at all of the stores she visited that day, the butt plugs were selling like hotcakes. There had even been a request made at one of the stores for a larger size. All the stores carried four different sizes of plugs, and the largest was . . . Brett pulled a ruler out from the desk and measured the extra large model. A six-inch diameter. Someone wanted one larger than that? Brett stared at the wall, then realized she really didn't want to imagine a larger one in use. She looked at her watch. She was supposed to pick Allie up from school. She grinned at the thought of Allie and forgot all about butt plugs.

Allie had told her to meet her in the front entry of Sterling Heights High School, but there were only parking lots to either side of the tremendous brown structure, and it looked like there were two front entries, so she parked off to one side and entered the closest one. When she didn't see Allie, she cut through the school to the other entry. She stayed inside rather than outside in case Allie was looking for her. She couldn't help but think how prison-like this windowless building was and briefly wondered what sort of things went on in here that they'd want to keep secret. She was glad she wasn't in high school anymore.

En route, she heard sounds of a scuffle emanating from one of the side halls and was about to keep walking when she heard Allie's voice.

It didn't take long to assess the situation. One boy had Allie pinned against a locker while two other boys waited their turn and one of their girlfriends egged them on. All of the boys had on varsity letter jackets. There were no teachers or other adults in sight.

"She grabbed my ass during bio!" the pock-faced girl screeched as the boy pounded Allie into the locker.

"Why the hell would I want your skanky ass?!" retorted a nearly breathless Allie, who looked incredibly sexy in a black leather jacket and tight blue jeans that showed off her long legs.

"Dyke bitch!" bellowed one of the other, obviously more creative youths. He had squinty little eyes, a shaved head and acned skin.

In four steps Brett was behind Allie's assailant. She grabbed him by the neck and threw him backward onto the floor in one swift movement. One of the other two charged her, but she quickly kneed him in the groin and shoved him back against the girl, then planted her foot in the chest of the grounded youth — the heaviest of the bunch, obviously a linebacker.

The third was taking no chances; he pulled a

knife. As he jumped forward, Brett jumped backward; as he slashed empty air, Brett pulled her gun. "Three-fifty-seven, don't leave home without it."

"Hey, babe, take it easy."

"Don't call me babe." She raised the gun level with his head.

"We were just teasing . . ." said another boy. "We're really friends with, with . . ."

"Allie," said the girl, glancing about for a way out.

"Yeah, we're real good friends with Allie."

Brett carefully aimed the gun at his groin. "Bang."

All four took off running in separate directions, each for himself.

Brett pocketed her gun just as a teacher stuck his head out of a classroom door. She grinned at Allie, who leaned against a locker with cool dispassion. Her T-shirt billowed enticingly around her breasts.

"Do I know how to clear the place, or what?"

"I could've handled it."

"I know you could've," Brett said, taking Allie's hand. "But I didn't want Assholes Anonymous to make us too late."

"Is that thing real?" Allie asked.

"No, in all reality it's a figment of your imagination."

"Smart ass."

"Better than being a dumb ass — I'm parked off to the side," Brett said as Allie went to the front of the school. "Have you ever thought about switching schools?"

"And have it all start again — with no friends on my side? Are you fuckin' nuts?"

"I just hate to think of anything happening to you . . ."

"Don't worry. That was just a bunch of bored, post-season football players and one girlfriend trying to make them all jealous."

"They're all dating the same girl?"

"Got me. I've never bothered trying to figure it out."

Brett looked at Allie as she opened the car door. "You know, you really are adorable."

Allie laughed. "Just get in and drive. I'm starving."

"Is the Backstage all right?"

"Yeah, that'd be great," Allie softly replied, glancing over at Brett.

Unlike most major cities, Detroit doesn't have a gay ghetto — its gay establishments are spread throughout all reaches of the city and its suburbs. The closest thing Detroit has to a gay area included two restaurants, two bars and the House of Kinsey, the bookstore Brett managed.

One of the two restaurants, the Backstage, was practically an institution. Its theatrical decor and varied menu attracted a straight lunch clientele from the nearby Chrysler plant in the daylight, and queer patrons at night. In the same building, owned by the same people, was also Footlights, a piano bar, and the Manhattan Room, a large room rented out for various occasions.

After they placed their orders, Allie looked up and again Brett smelled the musk of Allie's perfume. It hinted at her brain, like a thought not quite yet remembered. "What is that perfume?" Brett leaned forward and took Allie's hands.

"Eternity," Allie replied, as if pleasantly shocked by Brett's sudden gesture of intimacy.

"As in forever and ever?"

"Yes."

Brett grinned, warmed by the feel of Allie's hands. Allie touched Brett's class ring, which she wore on her right ring finger.

"College or high school?" Allie asked.

"College. I haven't taken it off since the day I graduated."

"And you never let anyone else wear it?"

"Never."

"Oh," Allie said, raising her eyebrows.

"So how long have you been out?" Brett asked as Allie toyed with the ice in her glass.

" 'Bout a year."

"Have you had many girlfriends?"

"A few."

"Did . . . Will I . . ." Brett began, not knowing how to ask such personal information on the second date, but still worried about the recruiting issue. Fortunately, Allie caught on.

"No, you won't be my first."

" 'Won't be your first?' " Brett mimicked with a sly smile.

"That's right."

"Pretty sure of yourself, huh?"

"What?" Allie asked, not understanding. "Oh," she added with a blush as it came to her.

Brett leaned over and put a hand on Allie's chin, tracing her lips with her thumb. They looked into each other's eyes, and the waiter came with their sandwiches.

"Save it for the bedroom, girls," he said as he

placed their orders in front of them. "You better watch out for this one," he told Allie with a wink. "She's a real heart-breaker."

"What did he mean by that?" Allie asked once the waiter left.

"He's just kidding."

"So you don't have a reputation."

"Not that I know of."

After they finished eating, Brett drove Allie home and they set a dinner date for that night. Brett said that she had to take care of a few things at work, but Allie would be at Brett's place at seven.

Brett headed for the House of Kinsey. Although Allie had said she didn't need saving, Brett wished someone had saved *her* when she was a teenager.

When she pulled up to the bookstore, two hustlers and a prostitute who were standing on the corner looked up, saw her and quickly took off down the street at a fast walk. They knew she didn't want them hanging around. Once they were out of sight, Brett headed into the store as a good-looking auburn-haired woman came out of the store, stopped and followed her back into the place.

Brett nodded to Geoff, the clerk, and quickly surveyed the brightly lit, clean store. She insisted that, because they sold a wide variety of porn and pleasure items, the place be kept immaculately clean — after all, this wasn't just an adult bookstore, they also carried jewelry, books and clean movies to appeal to a broad LesBiGay audience.

"Hey, Brett, the butt plugs are really selling like hotcakes lately," Geoff said.

Brett stared her reply at him.

"The woman behind you wants to talk with you — Kirsten, this is Brett."

Brett turned to face Kirsten, quickly sizing her up. She had very nice tits. Brett grinned and put out her hand. "What can I do for you?"

"Is there somewhere we can talk, in private?"

"Follow me." Brett led her into her rather small office and closed the door behind them. They stood just a few feet from each other.

"I've been told you can help people find, certain, ah, things they need."

"And just what sort of 'things' are you looking for?"

"There are a few things, besides a dark-haired, butch girlfriend." Kirsten grinned, unabashedly looking Brett up and down.

"Like?"

"Amyl nitrate."

Brett unlocked her desk drawer and pulled out a little brown bottle. She placed it on the desk and looked at Kirsten. "This one's on the house."

Kirsten took the bottle of poppers, her fingers brushing Brett's a bit longer than necessary. "Why, thank you."

"Anything else?" Brett asked with a charming grin.

"That was all I came in for, but now that I see you . . ." Kirsten intimated, putting her arms on Brett's shoulders. Brett rested her hands on Kirsten's hips. "Would you happen to be interested in a drink?"

Brett smiled, but before she could reply, there was a knock on the door.

"Rick and Frankie are here," Geoff said.

Kirsten turned and wrote something on a piece of paper she handed to Brett. It was her name and phone number. "Give me a call when you're a little less busy." Brett carefully folded and pocketed the paper.

"They're in back," Geoff said.

She went into the storeroom at the back and locked the door behind her. They often used the storeroom for extra conferences, or whenever it was convenient for whatever else they had in mind.

"Ralphie hasn't been seen since he left work last night," Rick said.

"I don' know who the deadbeats are, yet," Frankie said.

"But the shit floats out at night," Rick added.

"Do you need me?" Brett asked.

"Frankie'll take care of it, but I am worried about you."

"Me? Why?"

"I think some of the local small businessmen don't appreciate your playing on man's turf."

"You firin' me?"

"No, I just want you to watch it until we find out what's goin' on."

"Whatcha doin' tonight?" Frankie asked.

"Taking someone out to dinner."

"Fix her somethin' at home."

"Me? Cook? Are you nuts?"

"He's serious, Brett. Don't go out tonight, and make sure you keep your piece on hand at all times," Rick said, then added, "At least until we find out who's responsible."

* * * * *

When Allie arrived that night, Brett greeted her wearing an apron. She quickly led Allie to the kitchen where she deftly stirred the garlic and onions.

"You didn't strike me as the cooking sort," Allie said as she walked up behind Brett, sliding her arms around Brett's waist.

"Don't get used to it. It don't happen often." Brett swiftly sliced some mushrooms and added them to the pan on the stove.

"So why the special occasion tonight?"

"I need to stay by the phone — some of the stores have been having trouble and may need to get in touch with me."

"Some of the stores?"

Brett turned to take Allie in her arms, enjoying the feeling of nearness, the press of Allie's breasts and the warmth of Allie's body pressed against hers. "Yeah, I supervise a bunch of stores."

"What sort of stores?"

Brett pulled back to look at Allie and smiled. "I'll tell you over dinner."

Allie was surprised at how good the meal of chicken cacciatore, angel hair pasta and crescent rolls was, and said so.

"I learned how to cook because I got tired of Hamburger Helper," Brett explained. "And in college, I didn't have the money to go out to eat."

"So what is it you do for a living now?"

"Have you ever heard of the House of Kinsey?"

"Yeah, it's a gay bookstore, down near Highland Park."

"Gay and lesbian. Anyway, I started off managing that."

"But you have a degree."

"Which doesn't help much in a tight job market. I was out there trying to compete with guys with ten or twenty years' experience who were willing to work for the same salary."

"Oh, yes, corporate downsizing. About the only places hiring are fast food restaurants."

"For minimum wage." Brett suddenly realized that none of her own peers at Pershing would've been able to keep up with this conversation when they were seventeen. Too many of them were busy trying either to help their families survive or to be the biggest badass around to pay much attention to any of the reasons they were where they were.

"No, actually, you're wrong there. That McDonald's is hiring over the minimum wage shows that the minimum's set way too low," Allie said, meeting Brett's hazel eyes.

"Is that where you work? McDonald's?"

"Yeah, flipping burgers with my friends. It gives me some extra spending money."

"I've flipped a few hundred thousand burgers myself," Brett said to ease Allie's apparent embarrassment over her employment. Allie grinned her appreciation. Brett leaned back with her wine. "I ended up taking the job managing the House until I could find something better."

"When was that?"

"A coupla years ago. And, as it turned out, the fellow who owns it also owns several other stores and businesses." She wasn't sure if she wanted Allie to know just what it was she did.

"So he asked you to run it all for him?"

"Basically. I supervise the stores, leaving him free to take care of other matters — like expansion," Brett said, hoping that would end that.

"They're not all gay and lesbian, are they?"

"No, they're not."

"Then what are they?"

Brett thought about lying, but lying only led to more lying, and then where would it all end? "Adult businesses."

"Like . . . ?"

"A bunch of adult bookstores, a theater and a distribution service. That's why I carry a gun — some of them are in really bad neighborhoods and I often have to transport cash to and from them."

"You're talking about pornography, right?"

"Yes."

"But . . ." Allie apparently didn't know what to say. She looked baffled. Brett guessed that Allie thought pornography was a Bad Thing and wondered why a woman was mixed up in it.

"I know, a lot of feminists have problems with it — but the toys and novelties are just that — toys and novelties meant to help people explore and enjoy their sexuality. They're not necessarily a mode of evil. And, if you really think about it, the safest sex of all is with yourself."

"But what about the way those mags make women look?"

"I don't think pictures can cause the violence and

degradation all on their own. Plus, those things have been around a long, long time. People are just pinning the blame on the easiest thing available — like they do when they're homophobic." Please, she thought to herself, please don't let this disgust her.

"Is all this legal?"

"Yes. We do have to be careful, though. The laws vary from area to area. For instance, watersports are illegal in Warren."

Allie stared at her for a moment. "You're not talking about swimming and skiing, are you?"

"No. And before you ask, just believe me when I say that you don't want to know what watersports are." Allie grinned at this.

"You don't do anything with kids, do you?" Allie asked, looking worried.

"Hell no! I laid down the law with Rick on that one. If he ever gave me anything to do with kids, I was outta there. I do have some principles."

After dinner, Brett was relieved when Allie let the topic slide from her employment. They sat on the couch, watching a movie, and Brett slid her arm around Allie's shoulders. Allie leaned in a bit closer and snuggled up to Brett. Brett leaned down and gently ran her lips over Allie's. Her free hand found its way to Allie's waist, and she drew the young woman in closer.

Slow down, Brett thought. She's young. There's no need to rush things . . .

It was 11:30 by the time Allie got home. Both her parents were in the family room, just finishing watching the news. Maggie Sullivan was knitting, and John was still reading the same book from the night before. She gave them a sheepish look when she entered, and her dad responded by glancing at his watch and cocking a bushy eyebrow at her.

"Is this becoming a habit, kitten?" he asked.

"I'm sorry, it won't happen again," Allie replied, wanting to just sneak off to her room but knowing she had to say something more. "I was . . . I went to Brett's for dinner and a movie." There, she said it. She suddenly hoped her father had filled her mother in.

He seemed to read her mind. "I hope you don't mind, I told your mother earlier today. I needed to talk it over with someone."

Her mother looked up at her. Allie had never before noticed how beautiful her mother still was. The wrinkles did nothing to mar her fine features and she had always kept her slender figure. Even though she refused to dye her hair since it turned white in the past few years, so she was often mistaken for Allie's grandma, the white crown only increased her individuality and dignity.

Her mother opened her arms and Allie went into them, burying her face against her mother's breast. "Honey," her mom said, gently stroking Allie's hair. "I watched you grow up, saw you with all your friends, even Cybill over the past few years. I had hoped I was wrong, but it doesn't really surprise me."

Allie found herself crying.

"Now, are you going to tell us about this Brett of yours?" her father asked.

* * * * *

It was dark when Frankie and Brett pulled up into the potholed lot and parked behind the dark blue sedan with the busted window and crash marks along both sides. They got out of the Thunderbird, glanced at each other, checked that their guns were chambered and knives were accessible, then headed across the uneven pavement into the dingy bar whose name, etched in peeling paint on the inside of the dirty front window, was barely noticeable.

Frankie had always prided himself on being able to handle things. He made sure his brothers survived the rough Chicago neighborhood where they grew up. He handled the fellow who killed his sister several years ago. And he knew how to get out of town to make sure he lived to tell about it.

He met Rick DeSilva shortly after he moved to the Motor City just over five years ago. Someone was trying to mug Rick in the parking lot of a sleazy bar where Rick was trying to recruit dancers. Rick and Frankie became quick friends, and Frankie was just the sort of guy Rick was looking for to help him with the businesses he had recently inherited from his father.

Frankie liked Rick. Rick had ambition, and Frankie was perfectly happy to ride on his coattails. Frankie knew he wasn't smart, but he was smart enough to know who to talk to, who to threaten, who to bribe and who to kill. He had no qualms about killing. He figured the people he killed deserved to die. They had done something wrong, so they'd pay for it. Sometimes these people were double-crossers, sometimes they had big mouths, sometimes they threatened the wrong people, and sometimes they were just plain assholes, like the fellows who had threatened Storm.

Storm was important to Brett, and therefore important to Frankie. Brett and Rick were Frankie's only friends, so he protected them and stood for what they believed in. They were also the only two people on the planet who knew Frankie was gay. Brett didn't care, because she was too, and Rick didn't care because it didn't interfere with his work. The guys Frankie fucked never became close, because Frankie didn't want them to. He didn't like being a fag, so he chose to play the role he was intended to, that of the big protector and handler, and fucking guys was just something he did when he was horny.

And tonight, Frankie was in his role of handler. Rick had told him to handle the Ralph situation, and that's what he was doing. He had to find out who gave the orders, how they found out, and make sure it never happened again.

Frankie had spent the day asking about Leo and Johnny, and that had led him and Brett to this particular pool hall. He patted back his hair, adjusted his collar and entered the vile domain. Brett waited in the doorway, not wanting to give their identity away too early in the game.

The inside of the bar was as gloomy as the night had been on this unlit street. Inadequate lighting did very little to help, and years of cigars, cigarettes and rarely bathed patrons gave the place an omnipresent odor.

"Jack, straight up, beer chaser," he growled to the bartender.

"Four bucks," the bartender growled back and set down the shot and beer.

Frankie pulled out a ten and placed it on the counter. "Where's Leo and Johnny?"

"Leo and Johnny?"

"Yeah, I noticed their beat-up shitwagon out front."

"Over there." The bartender gestured across the room to two guys playing pool.

"Why don't you clean those glasses over there for a bit." Frankie nodded toward some glasses behind the bar and laid two hundred-dollar bills on the counter.

"They are looking a bit splotched." The bartender pocketed the money and turned to the rows of bottles that stood as silent sentries behind the bar. Frankie swaggered across the room.

"What?" Leo said when Frankie leaned on the table with its dirty green surface.

"I don' like your attitude." Frankie yanked Leo off his feet by his shirt collar and turned just in time to grab the custom-made pool cue Johnny was swinging toward his head. He pulled in on the cue, dragging Johnny with it, before shoving him back on the ground.

"Hey, we don' want no problems." Leo squirmed for his gun. Frankie pulled out his own and held it against Leo's temple. Brett walked up and surveyed the scene.

"Yeah, neither do I," Frankie said, looking at both Leo and Johnny, "but I understand you've been fuckin' with a friend a mine."

"Total misunderstandin', I'm sure," said Leo weakly. Johnny stood up shakily, sweat glistening on his black skin, obviously unsure of what to do.

"I don't think so," Brett said, pulling her gun out to rest by her side.

Frankie looked at Leo and Johnny. "Now they recognize you," he said to Brett. He suddenly threw Leo against Johnny, which knocked them both off their feet. Frankie quickly moved to stand on their chests and leaned down to look them both in the face, his gun still at the ready. "So you're gonna tell me who gave you the order," he growled.

"We don' know nothin' . . ." Leo glanced between Frankie, Brett and Johnny.

Brett leaned in and swatted him with the barrel of her gun, ripping a shred across his forehead. "Wrong answer! Thank you for playing!"

Frankie looked at Johnny. "You can give me the right answer, or else I'll get real angry, and you wouldn't like me when I'm angry."

"Jack O'Rourke."

"Good boy." Brett stood and nodded. "Now who told him 'bout Ralph?"

"I dunno," Johnny began and quickly added, "Really — I dunno — but Leo might." Leo was starting to come to.

Frankie grinned in his face. "Who told Jack 'bout Ralph?"

"Fuck."

Frankie brandished his gun in Leo's face. "I ain't askin' again."

"Some guy down at the Paradise."

"What was his name?"

"I dunno — Fred, Ned, somethin' like that."

"Thank you so much, you boys have been most helpful," Brett said.

"There's a message we'd like you to give Jack O'Rourke from Rick DeSilva," Frankie said, just before he jumped on their rib cages, enjoying the sound of breaking bones. A few minutes later, as they climbed into the car, Frankie could still practically hear Leo's and Johnny's screams.

The next day, Frankie beat the shit out of Ted and Brett told him that if they ever saw or heard from him again, he was dead. He got the message and left town.

Frankie wanted to take care of Jack O'Rourke, but Rick decided that that would mean war, and he didn't want to bite off more than he could chew. They decided to wait and see if Leo and Johnny carried the message to Jack.

Thirty-two-year-old Homicide Detective Sergeant Randi McMartin came in from her unmarked car and leapt up the station stairs to her lieutenant's office while her partner ran across the street for some doughnuts. She hoped he picked up some of those chocolate-frosted cream-filled ones she liked — of course, the moron would probably purposefully not get any, just to piss her off.

When she entered, Lieutenant Stanley Dzickowski, who was called Stas by those who knew him, stood with his back to her at his credenza, studying a stack of papers. A slender man dressed in a khaki suit, with glasses and short, thinning, dark hair leaned against the desk and wrote in a spiral-bound notebook. He looked up when Randi entered.

"Lieutenant?" Randi asked nervously, looking around for any other clues as to why she had been called here.

Stas turned around to face her. His white hair was neatly combed, but his heavyset body seemed to droop. His normally robust attitude was gone, replaced instead by one that made him look far older than his 50-odd years.

"Randi McMartin?" the nervous little man asked, straightening up to his full height, as if in response to Randi's 5′6″ frame.

"John, can you leave us alone for a moment?" the lieutenant said.

"But . . ."

Stanley Dzickowski was a man used to having his way. It only took John a few moments worth of his cold stare to realize that he really had no choice in the matter. When he left the room, Stas walked over, closed the door and turned to face her. "Randi, we've found your brother . . ."

"Oh, that little fucker — what'd he do now? I'll kill him for all he's put us through . . ." Randi paced and flipped her key ring around on her finger, angry at her brother's irresponsibility. He never cared what he put her or the family through, just did whatever the hell he wanted to, then expected her to bail him out every time.

"Randi," Stas said, putting out an arm to stop her. "It's a little too late for that." Randi looked up at the big man and fear dribbled down her spine. He read the look in her eyes. "They found him this morning in an abandoned warehouse on Cass."

"He's dead?"

"Yes. I'm sorry, Randi."

The words echoed through her mind — how many times had it been her saying those exact words — trying to show an unfelt empathy for the families, lovers, survivors of some auto accident, some attempted robbery, some drive-by shooting? Now she understood what those blank looks actually meant. She thought she should cry, but she couldn't feel anything.

"He was found with a —" Stas paused while he consulted a sheet of paper on his desk. "With a Robert Myslakowski. Although the autopsy results ain't in yet, it looks as if the cause of death to each was a gunshot sustained to the head." He paused again, as if wondering whether he should tell Randi anything else.

"A single shot?" she asked, looking up from the floor and into his deep brown eyes.

"A single shot did in your brother, but Myslakowski had a broken arm and ribs, a shot in his shoulder and two more to the head."

Randi glanced about at the squalor of the office, her world practically swimming before her eyes. The floor was filthy. Actually, it was beyond filthy, the tan tiles permanently ingrained with dirt forced into its grout from years and years of pacing. Papers overflowed out of the dark green metal trashcan. The puke-green filing cabinet was so overloaded its drawers wouldn't even properly close. The two windows along the far wall were so nasty she couldn't even really tell what sort of day was outside. The walls were darkened by years of cigarette smoke.

All around her was filth and decay, and it didn't just stop at the walls of this office. Her beloved Detroit was going down, fast. It wasn't the same town her parents had come to so long ago. Hell, it wasn't even the same place she had grown up in. Whatever happened? As if she didn't already know . . . It was the entire reason she had become a cop.

She looked up at Dzickowski. "Do they know anything else?"

He shrugged. "I'm sorry, Randi, but it looks like a mugging. Both your brother and Myslakowski were cleaned out — no ID, cash or credit cards, even their watches were taken."

"No, not just a mugging. No."

"Randi." Stas reached out and put a beefy hand on her shoulder. Randi looked up in surprise, it was the first time he had ever touched her. "It happens every day, we both know it — it's what we're fighting against. It just doesn't seem like it's possible when —"

"I'm sorry." She pulled away and pushed her hands back through her short hair. "I'm not just gonna let this go."

CHAPTER 8
Christmas

Christmas Eve Allie had to deal with her extended family. Brett wasn't quite ready to meet Allie's parents nor were they ready to introduce Allie to the entire family as a lesbian, so she couldn't bring Brett along. Storm, on the other hand, was very excited when Brett told her she was going to spend Christmas Eve and Christmas morning with her.

When Brett arrived after work on the 24th, Storm

had already picked up a tree and made the eggnog, but Brett had to figure out how the two of them were going to get the towering, eight-foot tree into the house and into its stand.

Once that trauma was over, they decorated it together while listening to Venus Envy's "I'll be a Homo for Christmas"—joking, giggling, laughing and drinking eggnog all the way, even when Brett, in all her butch bull-headedness, decided not to test the lights before putting them on the tree.

Although the ornaments were simple — some homemade, some from fast food restaurants as premiums when they purchased books of gift certificates, only a few store-bought — they augmented them with candy canes, and the entire combination came together with a soft red skirt below. Twinkling multicolored lights glittered near strands of silver in the middle and a brilliant star was perched on top. All in all, it granted the entire room a much beloved feeling.

After it was all done, they drank some more eggnog and cuddled on the couch. Brett liked the fact that she didn't have to put up any façades for Storm. She knew Storm loved all sides of her and that was all that mattered.

A while later, Brett went out back and brought in a few logs for the fireplace. As Storm prepared kielbasa and pierogies from Hamtramck — boiling the kielbasa in beer, then broiling it slightly till it was brown, and frying the cheese-filled pierogies with sauerkraut — Brett set about building a roaring fire to take the chill off the cold winter night.

"Mmmm . . . smells good." Brett entered the

kitchen and opened a bottle of wine with an asso, a two-pronged instrument that allowed her to open a bottle of wine without destroying the cork.

"The man at the shop told me this was the only way to cook it." Storm checked to make sure the fresh kielbasa was cooked all the way through.

After dinner, which they ate by candlelight in the dining room, they went back to the family room and Storm put in a videotape of *It's a Wonderful Life*, which they watched while cuddling on the couch under an afghan while the fire blazed away.

"Have you ever wondered what the world would be like without you?" Brett asked Storm after the movie.

"No, but I've worried about what it would be like without you," Storm replied. Brett wrapped her arms around her and they went to bed, where they made love for hours.

The next morning, Brett woke Storm early so they could open their presents.

"I swear, Brett, you can be such a little kid sometimes."

"Aw, but I wanna see what Santa left!" Brett handed Storm the fluffy fur robe she had given her last year and led her to the tree. En route, they passed a shelf to which, during the night, a stocking with Pamela's name on it had been attached.

"When did you get a chance to do this?" Pamela/Storm asked.

"I didn't — it must've been Santa," Brett said, her eyes wide with feigned amazement.

"Then why didn't he leave one for you?"

"Either I was a really bad girl, or he's a sexist pig."

Storm laughed and hugged Brett before pulling down the stocking filled with her favorite treats, from little chocolate Santas and Christmas M&M's to Ribbon Candy and Raspberry Stuffies from Sanders. She unwrapped a chocolate ball and placed it near Brett's lips. Brett grabbed it, and the tips of Storm's fingers, with her mouth. Storm gradually pulled her fingers out of Brett's mouth and softly moaned.

"You'd better stop that, or else we're not opening the gifts," she said.

"Why not?"

" 'Cause we'll be goin' back to bed."

"Decisions, decisions, decisions . . ." Brett pulled Storm into her arms and then down to the floor.

"Open this one first," Brett said a few minutes later, handing Storm a package. They were sitting cross-legged on the floor near the tree. Storm opened the brightly colored paper and squealed in delight at the hand-knit sweater she found.

"Oh, Brett, it's beautiful!" she said as she squeezed Brett. "Now you." She handed her a package.

"You shouldn't have." Inside she discovered three silk ties.

"Yes, I should — you have awful taste in ties, Brett."

She and Storm continued back and forth until they were surrounded with piles of tissue and wrapping paper. Brett finally handed Storm the last package and eagerly watched as she opened it.

"Oh, my God," Storm said in disbelief when she pulled out the gold and diamond heart necklace. "It must've cost a fortune. I don't know what to say."

"I had ulterior motives," Brett said, trying to

relieve the tension of the moment. She knew Storm would never be able to afford something like that either for herself or for Brett. She slid nearer to Storm and whispered, "I want you to go change and come back wearing only that."

Later that day, after a leisurely brunch with Storm, Brett went home to meet Allie. She didn't tell Storm what she had to do, but figured Storm had suspicions. After all, even in her line of work she usually got Christmas Day off.

Brett barely had time to turn on the tree lights, change and put on Christmas music before Allie arrived, looking lovely in a blue cashmere sweater and gray wool skirt. She put a bag on the floor.

"Femming up, eh?" Brett asked as she kissed Allie. Although Allie was definitely a femme, she usually didn't dress quite this nicely.

"God, I hate dealing with all the relatives."

"Don't say that."

"What's appropriate, what isn't, and how you should talk, act and dress is all so damned annoying. I just want to be who I am."

"Oh, honey," Brett took her in her arms. "I'm so sorry for you, but now you can just relax."

"I know." Allie sat on the couch and took off her pumps. Brett sat next to her and admired her nylon-covered legs.

"You do look good in that, though."

Allie turned to her and kissed her full on the lips before the warm glow Brett's compliment had given her could show. "Don't get used to it." Brett ran her hand the full-length of Allie's leg, enjoying the silkiness of the stockings. Allie took her hand into her own and looked at her. "I hope you weren't too lonesome last night."

"Nah, it wasn't too bad. I watched *It's a Wonderful Life.*"

"I wish you'd tell me what was so bad about your family."

Brett looked into Allie's eyes and came as close as she ever had to telling anyone about the horror of her youth, but knew that she couldn't. "Let's just say I don't care much for traditional family values."

Allie ran her hand down Brett's cheek. "My parents really do want to meet you, though."

Brett grabbed Allie's hand and kissed it. "I know." A part of her wanted to meet them too, and thank them for being so kind to Allie. But another, larger part just couldn't trust the way they'd treat her. She quickly turned on her charm and looked eagerly at Allie. "Presents!"

"For a big badass, you can be such a little kid." Allie retrieved the bag she had left by the door while Brett ran over to the tree and grabbed Allie's presents, all wrapped in different paper. Allie would never know that the wrapping paper was identical to those used for Storm's gifts.

"Open this one first." She gave Allie a package. Allie tore through the paper and opened the box. It held a key on a key ring made from her name.

She glanced up at Brett. "Is this what I think it is?"

"You can try it if you want to be sure."

An hour later, when they were almost done exchanging gifts, Brett sat back against the couch and took Allie in her arms, running her hand over Allie's silky tresses.

"I've never really believed in God," Brett said. Allie sighed softly against her chest. "I mean, I hope there's something after death, but I'm not quite convinced."

"I know what you mean."

"I do believe in the soul, though. These scientists keep telling us that we're only made of about two bucks' worth of chemicals, and I just ain't buying it. I think we're more than that."

"I hope so."

"I think there's something deep inside of us — a soul — that makes us who we are. And I think that we wander around through life looking for our soulmate."

"Soulmate?"

"This person touches you deep down inside, and you don't know what it is about them, but you know you belong together."

"How do you know when you've found your soulmate?"

"You just know." Brett hugged Allie and kissed the top of her head. "Hang on a second, babe."

She stood up and left the room, then returned with one last package. Inside the foil wrapping was a box that Allie gingerly opened. There lay a gold and diamond heart necklace. She was clearly dumbstruck.

"I want you to leave the room and come back wearing only that," Brett whispered in her ear.

CHAPTER 9
Taking Care of Business

A few days later, Randi stared at the theater across the street from her parked car. That was the last place her brother had been seen on the fateful night so long ago. She flipped her key ring around on her finger.

This once-beautiful building falling into disrepair in its new identity as a porn theater did not surprise Randi, for she saw it every day. Once-gracious and stately homes, austere buildings and monuments, immaculate and safe parks — all were turning toward a new identity as part of the crime, filth and destruction her city was becoming. This building was merely another fatality.

As a homicide detective she had been able to do some work on the case before she had to throw it into the pile of unsolved murders. She could only justify so much government expense on the one case, especially since departmental cuts had meant an increased caseload for all the detectives. The murders never decreased, only the number of cops did. She was lucky they had allowed her to work on a case in which she had so much personal interest.

Her brother had a history of drug abuse, petty larceny and other offenses, as had Robert Myslakowski, the man whose body had been near his in the warehouse. Even though Myslakowski came from a wealthy family, the police could only do so much in locating his murderer, particularly because it seemed as if they had met with a random act of violence.

Danny had promised her that he was changing his ways, starting over. She shouldn't have believed him. The drugs had so corrupted him that he didn't care how he hurt her or their parents. Their parents who had worked so hard trying to keep the family happy. Only second-generation Americans, they had both worked trying to make ends meet while raising their five children.

Danny was five years older than Randi. She loved her older brother and remembered the days when they were growing up and he'd give her piggyback rides around the park, or make sure that nobody beat her up. The entire time they were growing up he had kept her out of trouble and now she had failed to do the same for him.

He must've been about eighteen when he started his decline. Up until then, he had been a good son, a good brother. Since then, he had gotten into trouble time and time again. She didn't know what happened, he'd never talk about it. She guessed that he just fell in with the wrong people, people who convinced him there was an easier way, a way to make it without working. She had thought her years of work were finally helping, but then this happened.

It had been a little over a month since Randi had found out about the murder and, between her official casework and what she was able to do on her days off, such as today, she had discovered that the two men had spent a few of their last hours at the theater she now watched. She had reason to believe something had occurred on that night between her brother and one of the dancers, but she couldn't find anybody willing to say just what. All she knew was that the trail grew cold after they left that night.

She knew her brother and Robert went there often. She had also discovered that the owner of the theater, Rick DeSilva, had a history himself. Not that they had ever been able to prove anything.

She stared out her windshield and watched, knowing she would eventually figure out what happened that night. She had known from the first it hadn't been a simple mugging and was even more sure of it now. Something happened, and she would find out what, and bring justice to her brother's murderer, regardless of how long it took.

* * * * *

Kirsten left the theater annoyed. They wouldn't tell her anything about when Brett was due in next. She had seen Brett driving down the street one day and followed her to the Paradise, where Brett went right into the office, greeting the dancers by name enroute.

She wasn't used to not being able to attract a woman. Brett was an enigma, cold on the outside with a strange passion in her eyes. She couldn't figure her out, why she wouldn't call. There had to be some way, damn it, or else Allie would never come running back to her.

She sat in her car, watching as a few dancers left. Men flocked around them, and the guard had to keep them at bay. Kirsten had watched a show and envied the way the men looked at the dancers, the control those women had over them. And she had seen one of the dancers make over $500 for an hour's work giving lap dances. That was the life.

Brett pulled Kirsten's phone number out of her day-runner and stared at it. Kirsten was an interesting counterpoint to both Storm and Allie, each in her own way sexy and attractive. Brett smiled as she remembered the way Kirsten's jeans hugged her curvaceous body, how her shirt had billowed around her large breasts, open just enough to show off her collarbone and hint at her cleavage.

Brett reached over and picked up the phone. Suddenly, she remembered the deep blue of Allie's eyes, then imagined Storm's voice proclaiming her love. She couldn't bring yet another woman in. Maybe she could've in the old days, but she cared far too much for Storm and Allie to do that to them now. She put the phone down, crumpled the paper and threw it in the trashcan.

CHAPTER 10
Friends

"Hurry up, or else we'll be late," Allie nagged Brett as she looked at her watch.

"Will you just chill?" Brett yelled out from Rick's office.

"Feeling a little henpecked?" Rick grinned as he took a thick manila envelope of money from Brett.

"Naw, I got her just where I want her." Brett leered back.

"Only place I want a woman is flat on her back with her legs in the air."

"Then you're missing some of the best things a woman has to offer."

"Oh, God, Brett. Don't go gettin' all weird on me."

"Hey, Allie," Frankie said, knocking on the door to the stockroom and waving at her on his way to Rick's office. "Brett, how can you keep letting her wait?" he said as he entered the office.

"She's shopping," Brett said.

"You'd better be takin' good care of her," Frankie whispered. He had taken an immediate liking to Allie, who clearly didn't feel a need to engage him in constant conversation. She was a lot like him, Brett thought.

"Just because I don't tell you every detail, doesn't mean I'm not."

As Rick and Frankie bantered back and forth, what with things going so much better now that some of the other boys in town had learned a bit more about Brett, Allie was no doubt browsing through the toy and video stockroom where she was waiting. Next door was Rick's office, and across the hall was the magazine stockroom.

Every time she came to meet Brett, Allie always left with something — whether it was massage oils and creams, magazines or a new toy or two. Allie clearly enjoyed the benefits of Brett's employment, and Brett was slowly teaching her to enjoy some variety in their lovemaking.

"You ready to go?" Brett walked up behind Allie and wrapped her arms around her while Allie flipped through the pages of a *Playboy*.

"Yeah," Allie said, kissing her.

"Want anything?"

"Not right now," Allie said.

"You girls have fun tonight." Rick grabbed his black leather briefcase and headed out.

Allie and Brett left the building and sloshed through the slush as they went to Brett's car. They were meeting Cybill and her girlfriend, Erin, for dinner that night.

"I want to live in California someday," Brett said as she opened the door for Allie. She silently hoped for an early spring to end the February dreariness.

"Someday," Allie agreed, although she'd confessed to liking the variety Michigan afforded — the autumnal colors, the clean, white snow drifts on Christmas morning, the cleansing showers of spring and the chirping of the first robin.

Cybill and Erin were already at the Backstage when they got there, even though the Backstage was just up the street a block or so on Woodward.

"What took you so long?" Cybill asked

"Business," Brett replied as she helped Allie out of her coat and into the booth.

"Just what is it that you do?" Erin asked after introductions had been made.

"I supervise the various establishments my boss owns."

"Really? What sort of places?"

Allie and Cybill laughed.

"You really don't want to know," Brett said with a grin.

"What's so funny?"

"Well, she manages the House of Kinsey," Allie began.

"And several adult establishments," Cybill finished.

"Really? That must be interesting."

"Erin here's so pure she won't even watch jeans commercials," Cybill joked.

"Cybill!"

"C'mon, Erin, y'know it's the truth," Allie said.

"Well, maybe we oughta fix that," Brett said with another grin.

"Maybe," Erin said, slowly giving Brett the eye.

After they ordered their dinners, Cybill said to Allie, "Are you still having problems with those jerk-offs at school?"

Brett looked at Allie.

"It's nothin' big. Don't worry," Allie replied.

"Is it those same assholes I met?" Brett asked.

"No, it's some new ones."

"Why don't I just —"

"Why don't you just let me deal with it? Okay? I'm a big girl now. I can take care of myself. Now, if you'll just excuse me, I gotta use the john." With that, she rushed from the table.

Brett began to follow, but Erin stopped her. "I think I can handle this better than you."

Erin went to the bathroom, and Cybill leaned back in her chair and asked Brett, "What did you do to them?"

Brett shook her head. "Just taught them some manners."

Just then, Kirsten entered the restaurant on the arm of another woman. Cybill stared across the restaurant at her.

"You know her?" Brett asked.

"Yeah, it's one of Allie's exes."

"Oh, really?"

"Why so interested?"

"No reason," Brett lied. She remembered the way Kirsten had come on to her.

When Allie and Erin returned, their meal was brought out. Allie explained that she thought the introduction of guns to the scenario may be asking for more trouble, and she was graduating soon, anyway.

After dinner, they had planned on seeing a movie, but Cybill jokingly remarked that perhaps they could give Erin her first adult experience, and Erin took her up on the deal, so they headed for the Paradise Theater, which was just down the street.

When they entered the dim auditorium, with its cheap cracked seats and indelible smell, the first dancer was leaving, already done with the lap dances.

From all sides music started to play, almost a white noise, which was invaded by a single trumpet that gradually swelled as more instruments joined its mellow strains. A human voice entered, beginning the voyage of Enigma, and set the tone for a very different dancer. Drums, pounding out their rhythm, led into chanting, which gave the song its religious air.

Storm slowly moved onstage, drifting to the chanting melody. Her body flowed to the voices, flowed to the beat that was its heart.

The men arose from their coma and began hooting and hollering as she started dancing.

Allie and Cybill were very interested, Erin shocked, and Brett was trying desperately to maintain dispassionate disinterest.

Storm glanced over the crowd as she seductively moved about the stage, taking in the many male gazes, acknowledging, however briefly, their existence. Her eyes momentarily met Brett's before she realized whom Brett was with. When she noticed the other women, she quickly looked away and focused instead on the top of the back wall, as if trying to keep her eyes off of Brett with these strange women.

She knew she could lay no claim on Brett, but she hated that Brett brought other women here to see her. And she couldn't keep her mind off the thought that Brett was probably sleeping with at least one of them, and knowing Brett, it was probably the blond. As the beat continued, as she slowly took piece by piece of her clothes off, she felt the gazes of these women upon her. She felt them staring at her. She brought her head down and around to stare at each of them in turn, slowly licking her lips. Her eyes met Brett's and she tried to mimic Brett's cool gaze but had to turn away.

As the beat played on, rocking the packed auditorium with its unearthly sounds, the audience began to sweat and squirm in their seats. Storm pulled off her g-string and tossed it defiantly to the floor. The four women watched. They watched as Storm, naked except for her heels, felt a faint sweat breaking out on her skin. She danced for herself, disregarding all others in the auditorium.

Allie leaned back and lit a cigarette, her eyes glued to the stage. Cybill mimicked her and Erin admired the speaker mountings on the wall. Brett stared at the floor, wondering how she ever got talked into this. She got up to leave when Storm picked up her g-string and came offstage to start the lap dances, but Allie pulled her back.

"I wanna watch this," she whispered. Erin and Cybill whispered between themselves. Suddenly, Cybill waved some money for Storm and bought Allie a lap dance.

Storm had not yet put her g-string back on when she took the money. She looked first at Brett, then at Allie, then lifted herself onto the arms of Allie's chair. Brett turned away, although she could feel Storm's calf brush against her arm. Allie turned bright red. Storm pulled Brett's head back to watch as she slowly moved about on Allie's chair, sliding her legs down so she straddled Allie. She put her breasts in Allie's face and placed Allie's hands on her legs, up her thighs.

"Do you like what you see?" she asked loud enough for Brett to hear. A groan escaped from Allie's lips in acknowledgment.

Storm's arms were around Allie's neck, her mouth at Allie's ear. Allie leaned back in her seat, no longer red with embarrassment. Storm moved her hips to the continuing music, and Allie's gaze drifted down her body, to the moist spot between her legs. Storm arched up and offered herself to Allie.

Storm pulled Allie's head back up and looked deep into her eyes. Brett watched as she met Allie's lips for a deep kiss.

As they left the auditorium, Erin asked Brett why she was so uncomfortable during Allie's lap dance.

"Well, I'm friends with a lot of the dancers, and it's tough to watch a friend do something like that," Brett lied. Actually, she was seething that Storm and

Allie both seemed to enjoy the experience so much. She tried to quickly maneuver the group out the door, but Erin spoke up.

"What's on the other side?"

"Just gay porno flicks."

"I've never seen one of those before."

So Brett was conned into giving the women a full tour of the establishment, destroying her plans for an exit before Storm was done with the lap dances. Hopefully, because the place was so packed with men, they would still have a chance to be gone by the time Storm was done.

Erin said she had never before looked at so much as a naughty magazine but had an "academic interest" in the subject. At first glance, she seemed appalled and sickened, but as she watched the movie, where the men ran and fucked uninhibitedly, doing each other in as many ways as they could think of, she squirmed. Brett smirked, watching as Erin moved closer to Cybill, who pulled her close with an arm about her waist.

When they returned to the office, Sal looked up at them. "Storm's done dancing, if you gals wanna go and visit."

Brett cast Sal an evil look, because now she no longer had an excuse to get away without introducing Allie to Storm. When they got to the dressing room, Storm was changing into a sweatshirt and jeans, preparing to go home. She stopped before pulling on the green and white Michigan State sweatshirt, which Brett had given her, instead turning to greet the women wearing only her jeans and a lacy white bra.

"Storm, I'd like you to meet Cybill, Erin and Allie," Brett said, trying to think of anything but

Storm in that bra, anything but Storm giving a lap dance to Allie.

"So glad to meet you." Storm shook each of their hands, but lingered with Allie. She looked into Allie's eyes. "Especially you."

Erin left the dressing room to peek in at the last dancer, and that was when Cybill grabbed a pen and jotted her phone number on a scrap of paper.

"If you ever need a friend to talk to," Cybill said, handing it to Storm with a wink. Storm took it, grinning and winked back at Cybill. Brett didn't miss the gesture.

"I'll keep you in mind." She looked at Brett and put the number in her purse.

As the four women left that night, Brett told herself she was going to have to sit down and have a talk with Storm. Cybill quietly imagined Storm's naked body pressed under hers, and Allie thought something strange was going on, though she couldn't quite place her finger on it. All she knew was that there was an undeniable energy between Brett and Storm. Even more undeniable, however, was how wet she was, and how much she wanted to make love with Brett that night.

CHAPTER 11

Lies and Deceptions

The next morning Brett was waiting at the door to the dressing rooms. "Just what were you doing last night?" she asked as soon as Storm arrived.

"My job," Storm replied impassively, pushing past her and into the dressing room.

"You knew they were my friends . . ."

"Yeah — I kinda noticed that."

"Then why the hell did you act like that with them?"

"Like what?!"

"A slut!"

"It's hard not to be a slut when you're not wearing any clothes."

"They wanted to see a porno theater, so I brought them to a porno theater. I didn't expect you to . . . to . . ."

"What? Take my clothes off? Strip for them? Make them hot?" Storm said slowly, assessing her. Brett was fuming. "Bet you got laid last night."

"That's not the point!"

"Then what the fuck is? You brought them here, to see me, so what is the fucking point, huh, Brett?" Storm turned away from her. "You used me."

"Storm!" Brett grabbed her by the arm.

Storm whipped around to face her. "I'll tell you what the fucking point is, Brett. You're just pissed because someone else got your woman wet. Your woman — that, that Allie woman," Storm spat as she ran out, leaving Brett staring after her.

Frankie came out of the office, grinning.

"And what the hell're you grinning at?"

"Whaddya think? I just got a B.J. from one a the boys."

"And I'm quitting my job and becoming a nun," she said, heading into the office. Brett knew Frankie never played at the theater.

"You ready for round two?" Frankie ushered in Kirsten. Her long auburn hair floated loosely around her shoulders, and she wore a long, black trenchcoat, open at the neck to reveal a silver cross that dove down toward her cleavage, red spiked heels and fishnet stockings. She brushed past Frankie to stand in front of Brett before she stretched her leg out on the desk, adjusting her garter. She slowly turned to look at Frankie.

"Uh, I think I gotta go beat somebody up," he said, leaving.

Brett flung open the door. "Frankie!"

Kirsten pulled her back into the office and shut the door. "I don't think we need him."

"Kirsten, look, I . . ."

Kirsten pushed her up against a wall, put her arms around Brett's neck and pressed every inch of her body against Brett's. Brett half-heartedly tried to pull away, but Kirsten pushed her tongue into her mouth.

The door opened and the morning clerk, Sal, entered, followed by Storm, who took one look at the proceedings and slammed the door behind her as she left. Brett pushed Kirsten away and ran to the door.

"Storm!" she yelled after her. "Fuck. Sal, go find Storm and bring her back here — but knock first!"

"Sure, boss," he said with a grin.

Kirsten looked at Brett and dropped the trench-coat.

"Get the fuck outta here."

"You don't like what you see?"

"Listen, bitch, I can only suspect what you're up to . . ."

Kirsten pulled Brett's hands down to her naked ass, then put her arms around Brett's neck, but Brett pulled away as she tried to kiss her again.

"You're Allie's ex and that's all I need to know."

"What does Allie have to do with this?"

"You don't wanna mess with me." Brett handed her her coat.

There was a knock on the door and Frankie

entered. He eyed Kirsten and gave her an evil grin. "Brett, you've really pissed Storm off now," he said.

"Frankie, can you get rid of this bitch?"

"Get rid of her?" Frankie replied with a toothy grin, giving Kirsten an awful gaze. Kirsten studied him and, slowly, put the coat back on.

"Not like that. Just get her outta my sight."

"Not like what?" Kirsten said, clearly beginning to realize Frankie's meaning.

"She buggin' you?" he asked.

"Very much so," Brett replied.

Frankie grabbed Kirsten and threw her over his shoulder. She screamed.

Brett walked up and cupped her chin. "Leave me the fuck alone, or I will fuck you up."

"Allie, there's something you really should know, can you meet me at the Backstage at six?" Kirsten said into the phone.

"What is it now, Kirsten?"

"I can't tell you over the phone." She was in the parking lot just outside the Paradise, which wasn't exactly a safe place for a woman dressed as she was. She turned around and noticed a black man and a white man leaning against a beat-up old Chevy watching her. Leaning back against the phone, she stuck one leg out, enjoying the effect she had on them.

Even if her body wasn't still warm from Brett's admiring glances and the feel of Brett's hands on her naked flesh, the silkiness of Allie's voice would have heated her in this cold weather. She was going to figure out some way of getting Allie back from Brett, there had to be a way.

Allie reluctantly agreed to meet her.

Kirsten walked over to her car, joyful in the knowledge of what she was going to do. She allowed her coat to fall open a bit for the men who watched.

Brett entered the dressing room and kicked out the other dancers. The place was a mess, and it didn't matter how much they cleaned or painted it, the dancers would always trash it as soon as they were done. It was impossible to keep clean, because so many different women came through there each month, and so many of them were such slobs. Bits of make-up were splattered everywhere: lipstick, blush, eyeliner. The vague smell of old marijuana and tobacco was barely concealed by the vast quantities of perfume so many dancers wore to hide the fact that they didn't regularly bathe. Brett glanced down and was disgusted to see a used douche lying in a corner near the trashcan.

"Storm."

"Leave me alone." Her area was always neat, although she had to fight to keep the other dancers out of her things.

Brett gently turned Storm around to face her. She cupped her chin and brought her face up to look at her. "Dear sweet Pamela . . ."

Storm pulled away. "Brett, don't."

"Pammy, don't do this to me. I'm sorry for what I

did." Brett pulled Storm's head to her shoulder and smoothed her hair. "I've got reservations for the Whitney tonight."

"Are you taking me or Allie?"

"Oh, baby, you know how much I care for you — don't make it a competition . . ." She cursed to herself as she realized just how tacky she sounded.

"Why? Because I'll lose?"

Brett didn't know what to say. She thought both Allie and Storm needed time and she also knew she could be very controling. She cared for them both very much, maybe even loved them both, but she thought she'd destroy them if she ever got too close. She didn't know what to say to Storm. She kissed her softly, gently, before running her lips over Storm's hair.

"Don't even think that," Brett whispered, and Storm's tense muscles slowly loosened as she gave herself over to Brett's embrace.

When Brett was pulling out Storm's seat for her at the Whitney, Allie was a few miles north sitting down with Kirsten at Footlights, the piano bar attached to the Backstage. Kirsten always said she liked its dim lights and low, soft music one could talk over. Although straights frequented the Backstage, they were rarely ever in Footlights.

Allie got right down to business. "So what is it I need to know?" She knew she was being bitchy, but really didn't feel like playing with Kirsten anymore, especially not since she had found Brett, a woman she knew she could trust. She could no longer understand what she ever saw in Kirsten.

"God, you look beautiful."

Allie looked away. Just what she was afraid of. Kirsten could be charming when she wanted to. "Is that what all this is about?"

"No, unfortunately not."

"What's that supposed to mean?"

"As much as I enjoy looking at you, that's not the reason I called."

"Then what is?"

"I . . . I've been seeing someone, and I found out something today . . ."

Allie's stomach dropped. "You don't have AIDS, do you?"

"No! No, nothing like that."

"Then what is it?" She knew she should've followed her better judgment and not agreed to meet her.

"I was visiting her work at today and someone saw us together and your name was mentioned . . ."

"Who?"

"I think her name was Storm."

"You're seeing Storm?" Kirsten wasn't making any sense, what was this leading up to? Another of her little games? Couldn't she get the hint that Allie was happy with Brett, that Brett was everything she could ever want?

"No, Storm was the one that mentioned your name."

"Kirsten, cut the shit and tell me what's up."

"I've been seeing someone and I just discovered that she's . . . she's . . ."

"She's what?"

"Seeing you too."

"What?" Maybe Kirsten wasn't paying as much attention to her as she had worried about.

"Brett Higgins. I've been seeing her since, like, December . . ."

"You're telling me you've been fucking Brett Higgins?"

"Yes. Now, I know what you're thinking, but . . ." Kirsten began. Allie put her head down in her arms on the table.

Kirsten stood, as if to comfort her, then Allie sat up, laughing hysterically. "That is the most ridiculous thing I've heard!"

"Allie!"

"You stand about as much chance with Brett as Cindy Crawford does with RuPaul!" Allie stood. "Now, if you're done lying to me . . ."

"I'm not lying!"

Allie stared at Kirsten for a moment, shook her head and walked out. Didn't Kirsten have any boundaries? Allie had thought Kirsten had occasionally followed her over the past several months and now she was sure of it. Where would this obsession of hers end?

"So how'd the meeting go last night?" Allie was lying on Brett's couch watching a movie after dinner. They had ordered in for a pizza before popping a tape into the VCR. Brett lay behind her, spooning her. Her head lay cradled on Brett's arm.

"Okay," Brett replied, feeling only a little guilty.

They were supposed to go out the night before, but Brett had had to cancel in order to make up with Storm.

"Get a lot done?"

"Got 'em down a bit in price, and they're gonna change their policy a bit."

"Oh?"

"They usually just randomly pack cases, but I've got a guarantee that no more than one copy of each video title will be included in each case, which is nice. I can spread duplicates out among the stores, but that gets to be a hassle if I order a case for each store."

"Well, that's good, I suppose. Wouldn't want you overloaded on *Edward Penishands*."

"No, we wouldn't." Brett rolled Allie onto her back and kissed her.

Allie pulled away and looked up at her. "Have you ever heard of a woman named Kirsten Moore?"

"Kirsten Moore?" Even her conscience was beginning to doubt her own integrity. If she was innocent, why was she playing dumb?

"She has long auburn hair . . ." Allie said.

"I've heard that name somewhere before."

"Well, she's been bugging me since I dumped her."

"She's your ex?"

"Yeah."

Brett hit her head. "I've got it — kinda pretty, slender, big tits, a bit shorter than you?"

"What are you doin' lookin' at other women's tits?"

Brett pulled away and stumbled across her words. "It's not like . . . Well, I . . . They're just so apparent?"

"Brett . . ."

"I manage an adult theater, I'm used to looking at tits."

"Brett, about Kirsten?"

"Oh, she's the chick that's been bugging me since, shit, since right after I met you."

"Well, she told me the most ridiculous story about the two of you sleeping together."

Brett laughed. "She's been tryin', and I've just been ignorin' her."

Allie cuddled in closer, facing Brett. Brett held her close. She buried her face in Brett's shoulder. "It's nice to be with someone you can trust."

Brett was glad Allie couldn't see her eyes.

CHAPTER 12
Sex and Lies

Storm and Brett decided to spend a leisurely day at the Detroit Zoo, which was, ironically, located in Royal Oak. It was late May, and the weather was finally becoming dependably warmer. Storm laughed when Brett imitated first the monkeys, then the elephants. Brett liked taking Storm's mind off her many problems, and Storm liked getting Brett to goof off and act silly.

"What are you thinking?" Storm asked as they sat on the grass enjoying their picnic lunch.

"How beautiful you are."

"Sometimes I wish I wasn't."

"I hate it when you talk like that," Brett said, taking Storm's hand.

"I know, but I can't help it," Storm said, looking down. Brett lifted her face so that their eyes met. She was glad Storm would discuss anything that bothered her with her, but that didn't mean she had to be glad for what made Storm say those things. Brett put her hand on Storm's cheek and leaned forward to kiss her gently.

"Someone might see us," Storm said with a smile.

"Oh, no, someone let the queers loose! Better hide the gerbils!"

"Prairie dogs. They don't have gerbils in the zoo."

Brett lay back, enjoying the warmth of the sun. The park was very nearly empty since it was a weekday. Storm lay her head on Brett's chest, and Brett put an arm around her.

"I think," Brett began, "that next time we should go somewhere really different. I mean, the stores and the theater are a zoo themselves."

Storm propped herself up on her elbows and looked into Brett's eyes. "What am I going to do with you?"

"Take me home! Take me home!"

"Oh, no. I have to work tonight."

"Unfortunately. You could always tell the boss you're sick."

"I don't know if she'd believe me — you know what a hard ass she is."

"Real bitch, huh?"

"Of course, she may not notice."
"How could she not notice you?"
"I think she has a hot date tonight."
"Oh, God, Storm. Don't ruin today."
"So you are seeing Allie tonight."
"Yes."
"Does she know about me?"
"No. She doesn't."
"What would she do if she found out?"
"I don't know. I don't want her to find out."

Storm began putting away their picnic things. She looked up at Brett, who watched her with concern. "Have you told her you love her?" she asked, obviously afraid of the response, a tear forming in her eye.

"No," Brett answered truthfully, without hesitation. "Oh, God, Storm." She leaned forward to wipe the tear from Storm's face. She wanted to say the words now, to Storm, but couldn't. Instead, she held her, rocking her in her arms in the sun.

A few hours later, at 5:30, Brett was taking Storm to work and they decided to go to the House of Kinsey first. Brett opened the door for her and, as soon as they entered, she pushed her against a wall and began kissing her.

"Omigod! Such blatant homosexuality!" screamed Geoff, the clerk, from behind the counter where he was reading the newspaper.

When Brett turned to say, "Damned right," to the red-headed 19-year-old Geoff, she noticed Kirsten leaning on the toy display case, watching her and Storm.

Brett had the narrow, long store set up so that when you walked in, the first thing you saw was the jewelry case. Next to it on the right was the cash register, and to the right of that, angled slightly away from the door, was the lubricant case — they carried a wide variety of lubes, massage creams and oils and various other related items. The toy case was at a right angle from the jewelry so that you had to walk around the store a bit to notice it. Brett didn't want people coming into the store to have that as their first impression. Among other things, Brett wanted this to be a safe place for people to acquire such items — instead of having to go into the stores along Eight Mile where they would feel compelled to wear a trenchcoat and hat to hide their identities.

The toy case also completed the square around the cash register. As it was, if you were looking at the toys, all you had to do was look up to see whoever was coming into the store.

Storm noticed Kirsten at the same time Brett did. "What are you doing here?"

"Shopping."

Geoff shrugged before he returned to his newspaper.

Brett turned back to Storm. "Honey . . ." She was worried about what Kirsten had seen and heard.

"Excuse me," Kirsten said politely to Geoff, "but do you happen to have an ejaculating butt plug?" Storm and Brett turned to watch Geoff.

"Why, yes, we have three different models," Geoff said, jumping to the appropriate display case and laying out the models in question.

"How about an ejaculating, vibrating butt plug?"

Geoff looked across at Brett.

Brett whispered officiously in Storm's ear, "This is the year of the butt plug." Storm giggled and buried her head in Brett's shoulder.

"And would you happen to know —" Kirsten turned to look at Storm and Brett. "— if Allie Sullivan knows about that?"

"Who? What?"

Brett shot Kirsten an evil glare.

"Allie Sullivan? Brett's other girlfriend?" Kirsten said as she continued staring at Storm and Brett.

"I really don't think Allie'd give a shit," Brett said.

"You don't think she'd care you're gettin' it on with another woman?" Kirsten approached the twosome.

"I'm gettin' a little tired of you tryin' to start shit," Brett growled as Kirsten stepped toward her. She knew she had been caught by the person who desperately wanted to catch her. She also knew she had to get out of it.

"You're the one who started it."

"Y'know, I can't quite decide who the object of your psychotic fixation is — me or Allie."

"Watching out for friends isn't a psychotic fixation."

"When it gets to stalking it is." She knew she was cornered, and like a cornered animal, she was ready to strike at the slightest provocation.

"Squirm all you want to — you know I've got you."

"Got me what? Hanging out with a friend?" She didn't know what to do. She felt like she had when she was younger and her father eyed her before a beating. She'd never let herself be in that position again, never again.

"Looks like more than friendship to me."

"Kirsten, you can just go fuck yourself, because you ain't gettin' anything from me."

"Like I'd want your ass."

"Don't go trying to make something out of nothing. Storm is a friend — a very good friend, but a friend nonetheless." It was out of Brett's mouth before she knew it. Storm raced out before she could take it back. Brett felt out of control, realizing that, once again, she had blown it with Storm. "You bitch!" she yelled at Kirsten. She heard Storm's car start up. Brett grabbed the collar of Kirsten's windbreaker and pulled her off her feet. "You're gonna pay." Brett hauled Kirsten into the storeroom, threw her to the floor and locked the door behind them. Kirsten stood to face Brett.

Brett didn't know what to do, she was filled with the fear of losing Storm through her own stupidity, and with anger at Kirsten, who seemed to want to play God with her and Allie's lives.

"This room is practically soundproof — I could probably cut you up into little pieces and no one would ever hear a thing."

Kirsten strutted toward Brett. "Oh, big bad bulldyke threatening a lil' ole femme."

Brett grabbed Kirsten's arm. "Or I could let Frankie have his way with you. He'd like that very much."

"Frankie?" Kirsten pulled away. "You want to give

me to Frankie?" She looked up at Brett, letting a coy little grin slide across her lips as she again began to slip her arms around Brett.

"I don't even want to waste the time of day on you," Brett said and left.

Storm got to the theater and rooted through her dressing bag for the phone number. She knew she had put it somewhere. She glanced around the room and began viciously tossing other dancers' stuff to the side. She slammed her hand against the wall as tears ran down her face.

She had first fallen in love with Brett during one of Brett's nightmares, when Storm was the strong one and Brett let Storm hold her. That the strong and cocky Brett let her hold her made Storm feel like she had something worth giving. She knew she couldn't make Brett choose, she was too afraid she'd end up the loser. She knew Brett was cut in two — with half of herself wanting the wild life, and the other half wanting a white picket fence with two-point-five children and a dog. And Storm couldn't give her that, yet. But someday . . .

She didn't expect Brett to be monogamous, but to say that she was just a friend in front of other people. To put her down like that. After exposing her to her other girlfriend. Brett could've stopped the lap dance that night, but she didn't. Well, the hell with her. Two could play this game. She angrily wiped at her face.

Aah, there it was. Storm walked out into the lobby and picked up the phone, without cleaning it first, which was her usual habit.

"Hello, Cybill?"

CHAPTER 13
Guess Who's Coming to Dinner?

Allie had told her parents she didn't want to go to her high school prom. Instead, she wanted to go to the Affirmations youth prom with Brett, and Brett wanted to take her to the Ritz-Carlton in Dearborn afterwards. She had flushed with embarassment because it implied so much, but she didn't want to worry them by staying out all night, and she couldn't lie to them and tell them she was spending the night at a friend's house.

John and Maggie still had not met Brett, so they told Allie that they'd like to meet her first, especially since she'd been seeing her for so long.

Brett reluctantly agreed.

The night before the prom Brett arrived at the Sullivan residence with a bottle of Chardonnay to go with the chicken she had been told they'd be having for dinner. She noticed the freshly mowed and edged lawn, the colorful flowers and the well-kept exterior of the house, so unlike the house where she had grown up.

John answered the door.

"Hello, sir," Brett said, extending her hand. Allie had asked her not to follow her first instinct, which was to wear a suit, advising her instead to wear a white polo shirt, stone-washed jeans and white cross-trainers. She even took the cock-ring off her wrist.

"You must be Brett," John said with a warm smile. He wore neatly pressed khakis and a light blue polo shirt.

"It's a pleasure to meet you, sir." Brett forced herself to look at his eyes, which were so much like Allie's, instead of following her impulse to stare at the ground. Although she had an innate distrust of fathers, she immediately liked him.

"Please, call me John." So unlike her own father, who spoke mostly in grunts and was always either shirtless or wore a dirty white T-shirt and stained work pants.

Allie greeted her in the living room. "Hi, honey," she said, wrapping her arms around Brett. "It'll be all right," she whispered in her ear.

"So you're Brett," Maggie said.

"Yes ma'am," Brett replied, turning to face her. She paused briefly, then smiled. "I can see where Allie gets her looks from." Maggie was stunning, and Brett had never before noticed the looks of a woman that much older. Brett looked at Maggie, Allie and John, and could envision what Allie would look like ten, twenty, forty years from now. She liked the image.

"Here, let me show you around the house," Allie said, handing the bottle of wine to her dad and leading Brett down the hall. Brett was impressed with the house. Not only was it clean and well-kept, but the colors and furnishings were obviously carefully chosen and displayed a certain amount of sophistication and money. Things she had never known while she grew up.

In Allie's bedroom she glanced around nervously, not accustomed to feeling ill-at-ease. The smell of Allie, which pervaded the room, helped make her more comfortable.

"You look good," Allie said, straightening her collar.

"Your parents are really nice," Brett said, carefully looking about the room, putting together what she knew of Allie with what she saw. She smiled at the stack of textbooks on the desk next to the computer.

"Brett," Allie said, pulling her into her arms and kissing her.

Several minutes later they rejoined John and Maggie in the kitchen. Brett remarked on the aroma, then proceeded to question Maggie as to her recipes and methods. John watched approvingly.

"So Brett, tell me, what do you do for a living?" John asked when they sat down to dinner.

"I supervise several retail outlets."

"Oh really? And just what do you sell?" Maggie asked.

"A lot of different things. Part of my job is keeping track of what's selling and what's not and ensuring that we stay competitive, both with our products and prices." Brett glanced at Allie, who was smiling.

"She got her bachelor's degree in business from Michigan State," Allie said, apparently as eager as Brett to not have her parents further question Brett's employment.

"Oh really?" John said. "I'm a Michigan man myself."

"That's an okay school," Brett replied. "But M.S.U. was cheaper, offered me more money and I couldn't resist their honors college."

Allie smiled her thanks for Brett's diplomatic way of dealing with the two schools' long-standing rivalry.

John gave Brett a reappraising look and Maggie said, "Perhaps you could help us with Allie. She doesn't seem to want to go to college."

"I've already been trying, ma'am. An education is never wasted, and she should definitely not look a gift horse in the mouth," Brett replied, referring to the fact that Allie's parents were willing to pay for her schooling.

Allie sighed. Apparently this was not new ground to her. Brett knew Allie had only recently told her parents she wanted to go to the police academy and be a cop. She also remembered how hard it had been to pay her own way through school, working forty or fifty hours a week while going to school full-time.

"She could even be a criminal justice major," John said. "We just want her to know there are other options out there before she limits herself." He leaned forward, looking directly at Brett, obviously surprised to have found such an ally.

After dinner Brett insisted that she and Allie do the dishes while John and Maggie enjoy a drink. When they were done, Allie suggested a game of Trivial Pursuit. Brett walked up behind Allie and wrapped her arms around her. She was almost surprised to find herself doing so, but wanted to be close to Allie. Allie took her hands in her own, as if she were comfortable being with Brett in front of her parents.

Allie had mentioned that her parents joined P-FLAG, but Brett couldn't believe how understanding they were. It was like a dream. She suddenly realized she belonged here, she was accepted here. She could grow to love these people and wanted to be a part of them. This was what she had imagined when she was growing up, fighting her way through school and life in the city.

John pulled out a bottle of Glenfiddich while they played. Maggie continued to drink wine, and Allie drank Diet Pepsi. The game was challenging and fun, but Brett realized she was most interested in the relationships going on. She gradually felt easy and comfortable touching and holding Allie, and being touched by her.

But it was when she caught John looking at Allie with obvious love and affection that she understood her own relationship with Storm. She was trying to have the same relationship with Storm, trying to be her mentor, her protector, but with a sexual relationship. And that wasn't the way it was supposed to be. She could never be Storm's father, but she could be her friend.

She observed the relationship between John and Maggie and realized she wanted the same thing, the consistent love, happiness and understanding, with Allie. She turned to Allie and remembered her own words about soulmates.

She wanted to spend her life with Allie.

Randi sat down to dinner with her parents.

"I still want to know when you're going to bring some nice boy home with you," her mother said, obviously trying to keep her mind off more depressing matters.

"I wouldn't hold your breath," Randi replied, wishing that she could one day tell them the truth. Tonight was not the night, though. Tonight would've been Danny's thirty-eighth birthday. She knew her parents still kept Danny's room, as they did for all their other children. They always said that this was still their home, ready whenever they needed it.

"Have you found out anything else about Danny?" her father asked, clearly neither forgiving nor forgetting.

"No," Randi lied, not wanting to get her parents' hopes up. Even as she said it, she saw a tear on her mother's cheek, saw her father's hands tremble.

Actually, Randi had learned that Danny had a

thing for a dancer at the Paradise named Storm, and that Storm was dating one of DeSilva's lieutenants, a woman named Brett Higgins. Her sources told her that Higgins was very protective of Storm, personally beating up anybody who even looked at her cross-eyed. Randi figured she took it a little too far one night.

Her mother brought in dessert, a cake that even without candles or writing was clearly a birthday cake. Randi wondered if Higgins had ever known pain like the pain she put these two wonderful parents through.

The next morning Brett went to Storm's house. She let herself in and went to the bedroom.

"Mmmm?" Storm said when Brett sat at the edge of the bed.

Brett took her hand in her own and pushed stray hairs from her forehead. "Pammy."

"What is it, honey?" Storm asked, looking up at her. She was so lovely, so beautiful, so desirable.

Brett took both her hands in her own. She didn't want to do this, didn't want to hurt her any more than she already hurt. But it had to be done sooner or later. She knew the pain she had caused Storm and would continue causing her. She couldn't keep on seeing both women, not with what she knew: she wanted to be with Allie and this would only continue to torment Storm. Someone always had to be hurt. She looked away.

"What is it?" Storm sat up as if she knew what was coming.

Brett brought Storm's hand up to her lips. She kept her eyes focused on the graceful fingers, the smooth skin. "We can't go on like this . . ."

"What do you mean?" Storm sat up, her T-shirt outlining the beautiful body underneath, the curves Brett knew so well.

"We both know I can't be all you need me to."

"No, we don't."

Brett looked up into her dark eyes. Why couldn't she have it both ways? Why did she have to change anything at all? "I can't go on lying." She ran her hand down Storm's cheek. "Pam, you make me feel big and strong and competent . . ."

"I bring out the best in you."

"You make me feel what I want to feel and I want to make you forget all the shit you've been through, but we're not right for each other. I'll always be there for you, but you need someone who'll be faithful."

"This is about Allie."

"Yes and no. Honey, I care for you very much . . ."

"But you don't love me."

"You should know better than that." Brett lifted Storm's chin so their eyes met. "I love you, but not the way you want me to. It's like we hold each other back — we don't challenge each other." A part of her wanted Storm to fight for her, but another, larger part knew that for the first time in her life she really knew what she wanted, needed, longed for.

"Life isn't about challenges, Brett."

"No, it isn't. I hate the thought of losing you, but I can't imagine a future without Allie. I love you, Pam, but not the way you need me to."

CHAPTER 14
Till We Meet Again

Brett carefully pulled the ends of the short, burgundy tie around her neck, tying it into a bow tie. She wrapped the cummerbund around her waist and pulled on the tailed black jacket. She adjusted herself again and looked in the mirror. She smiled a slow, easy smile then grabbed the corsage from the refrigerator and went out to the waiting limousine.

Brett thought briefly of Storm, and the pain in her eyes when she left that afternoon. They had made love one last time, but she had been firm in her insistence that it was over. That was the way it had to be. She knew she was hurting Storm by being with Allie, but she couldn't stop. She knew she was with Storm not so much as a lover, but as a father, or, as the ideal father — a protector, guider and advisor. And she also knew that Allie would not understand her being with Storm, and she couldn't stand the thought of losing her.

Storm was going out with Cybill tonight. The date had been arranged before this morning. Brett wished she could feel only good things about this, but she was hurt that Storm had been planning this date even before the break.

She could finally understand what she had been putting Storm through. That was different now, though, and she liked the feeling that she'd never put Allie through the same painful feelings of rejection and betrayal.

Tonight was not a time to think of Storm with Cybill, though. Tonight was for her and Allie. This was the first night of their new life together, a life Brett was dedicated to. The sun was shining, the world was a bright, warm place. She and Allie were voyaging into a new phase of their relationship and Brett felt good about this.

When she arrived at the Sullivans', John greeted her and led her to Allie's bedroom, where Maggie was helping her finish getting ready.

Allie was dazzling in a short, light blue, off-the-shoulder cocktail dress. Her long legs were emphasized by heels, and her hair was elegantly done in a French twist. Resting lightly on her soft skin just above her cleavage was the necklace Brett had given her for Christmas.

She took Brett's breath away.

Maggie stepped back and looked at them. She wrapped her arm around John's waist. "You two look so cute," she said as if she couldn't believe it. John smiled approvingly.

They went out to the living room where, after a few tense moments, Maggie apparently gave in to her maternal instincts and began snapping pictures of the two. Eventually John led Brett out to the patio.

"Brett, I have to be honest with you, you're not quite what I was worried about when Allie told me she was gay . . ."

"But I'm not quite what you wanted, either." Brett finished his thought, trying to make it easier on him. He looked at her gratefully.

"Maggie and I discussed it last night and agreed that you seem to be all right."

Brett suddenly realized she was having a man-to-man talk with Allie's father. "I'll never intentionally hurt your daughter, sir."

"You'd better not, or else you'll have me to deal with."

"I think I love her."

John smiled at that and playfully punched Brett in the arm. "You take care of her."

When she and Allie climbed into the limo, Brett popped the cork on a bottle of champagne and looked at Allie.

"Just looking at you like that makes me horny," she whispered in Allie's ear. Allie smiled demurely and took the glass.

"You're such a romantic."

"The end of high school — you finally made it."

"Not quite yet — graduation isn't until next weekend."

"I think you can make it."

"All I know is, you'd better shape up or you'll be in trouble."

"And just what do you mean by that?"

"I know you don't just supervise the stores for Rick," Allie said, putting her arms around Brett's neck.

"*Moi*?" Brett nuzzled Allie's exposed neck.

"I don't know just what it is you people do, but you'll be in trouble when I'm a cop."

"Are you accusing me of illegal activities?" Brett kissed Allie's ear. Allie pulled back, raised her eyebrows and nodded. Brett grinned back and touched her lips to Allie's.

"Honey, I'd never do anything to hurt you," she said.

Storm's neighborhood, where Cybill picked her up for their first date, was a lot less elegant than the Sullivans', but these two women also had the feeling of voyaging into a new phase of life.

Cybill was excited about the date — Storm was good-looking, sexy. Although there seemed to be something going on between Storm and Brett, Cybill wasn't quite sure what it was. Regardless, she wanted Storm and was planning a night never to be forgotten.

When Storm answered the door, Cybill was

amazed at how good she looked in clothes, but she grinned not only at that, but also at her own foresight in telling Erin that she was going to be out of town the whole weekend.

The two women were both slightly nervous, but things were becoming relaxed quite quickly as Cybill drove to the Backstage. At the restaurant, Cybill secured a back, candlelit booth and the two women enjoyed the romantic gay atmosphere as they leisurely sipped their wine, talking about almost nothing at all.

"So have you known Brett long?" Cybill asked.

"She's one of the first people I met when I moved up here."

"Oh, where're you from?"

"Nowhere, really."

"So have you been dancing long?"

"Just since I moved here."

"Which was when?"

"A while ago."

"So Brett got you into it?"

Storm took one of Cybill's hands. "I came here to be with you, not to talk about Brett . . ."

Storm couldn't believe she was going out on a date with another woman. That she was planning to sleep with this woman to prove her point to Brett. She was going to make Brett realize that she really did love Storm, regardless of what she had said that morning.

In the beginning, Brett had always been romancing her: taking her to movies, dinner, sending her flowers, candy, jewelry. The first time Storm had seen Brett, there was electricity in the air: the way Brett looked at her, the way she smiled. And Brett was always there for her — when she was harassed, threatened or just plain scared. Since they had met, Brett was the only woman Storm had touched.

Of course, that was in the beginning. Back before Allie. Well, Storm would deal with Allie in her own way. She'd get her Brett back. And she'd get Brett to stop and look around her — begin to live life, instead of merely running from the past. It would be Storm who would unlock the carefree, happy Brett that now only surfaced on occasion.

Storm grasped Cybill's hand and kissed it. Cybill leaned over the table and kissed Storm on the lips. Storm fervently returned the kiss.

The limousine pulled up at the Whitney, an elegant old manse that was still an elegant old manse, located on Woodward mere blocks from the very worst part of the Cass Corridor — in fact, not far from a certain old warehouse on the Cass Corridor. Its ivy-covered walls echoed a more sophisticated time, from the fine linen tablecloths to the austere wine list and tuxedo-clad waitstaff.

After a nice, romantic dinner, Allie and Brett went to the prom where they were greeted with warm hugs and admiring glances. Theirs was the only limo in the lot when they arrived.

"Hey, look, Allie's got herself a sugar mama," a woman said with a wink as Brett opened the door for Allie.

"Who you callin' a mama?" Brett demanded while Allie grinned and gave her friend a hug.

They began to mingle, greeting and being greeted, drinking punch and eyeing other couples similarly dressed to the nines.

"Girlfriend!" screamed Mike. "I haven't seen you in forever!" He came flying up to throw his arms around Allie. "So this is the new woman?" he said suggestively, eyeing Brett up and down.

"Yeah," Allie said bashfully.

"Brett," Brett said, putting out her hand.

"Mike," he said, putting out his, which Brett grabbed and kissed. Mike grinned. "I like her," he said to Allie.

"So do I," Allie said, hugging Brett.

Brett was glad Kirsten hadn't been able to make it. She didn't need that extra frustration tonight.

The DJ started another round of music and they headed to the dance floor. Neither truly led nor followed as they bopped to the quick dance beat, but they were obviously a couple as they danced about the floor, surrounded by other queers. At this gathering, there was no nervous time while the boys tried to get up the nerve to ask their dates to dance — they had come to dance, and dance they would.

After the naming of the King and Queen, wherein the queen was truly a queen, the DJ started playing a few slow songs. Allie and Brett moved into each other's arms. Allie placed her head on Brett's shoulder and Brett held her as they swayed to Whitney Houston's "I Will Always Love You."

"Don't make promises you can't keep."

"I don't." Brett knew what she said was true, and

she knew that Allie suddenly, inexplicably, believed her. They looked into each other's eyes and Brett realized that she loved her, and always would.

They kissed. And kissed. And kissed.

When they finally left the prom a few hours later, a sudden summer shower had broken so they had to rush to the limousine to avoid getting soaked. They were one of the first couples to leave the prom, and they headed to the Ritz-Carlton in Dearborn, where Brett had gotten a room. In the back seat of the limo, Brett opened another bottle of champagne and poured herself and Allie a glass each. They drank with their arms entwined, spilling only a portion as they giggled.

"I love you," Allie said, looking into Brett's hazel eyes.

Brett smiled and pulled Allie close. "I have the strangest feeling you're telling the truth."

Storm and Cybill got caught in the sudden cloudburst outside Storm's house. As they ran in, Cybill caught Storm's arm and turned her to face her. She kissed her hard on the lips, until Storm's arms entwined around her neck, and they stood in the downpour kissing.

"We're getting drenched!" Storm pulled away from Cybill and ran to the house. Cybill caught her again on the front stoop.

"So?" Cybill said, again kissing her before she led her into the house.

"Make yourself comfortable, I'll get us some towels," Storm said.

Cybill looked around and turned on the radio, selecting a romantic station, WNIC, with its nightly dose of "Pillow Talk." She walked up behind Storm and nuzzled her neck. Storm moaned slightly and turned to her with a smile and a towel, which she wrapped around Cybill's neck before pulling her in for a kiss. Cybill leaned into Storm, her leg between Storm's legs. Storm groaned her reply.

Storm led Cybill into the bedroom and quickly began to undress her in the dark as they continued to kiss.

"Ooo, a tigress, are we?" Cybill asked as Storm pushed her back on the bed.

"I know what I want," Storm said, quickly undressing. She climbed on top of Cybill and straddled her. Cybill looked up, noticing the thin waist, the full breasts and the smooth curves of Storm's body.

"Then we're in luck, because I want the same thing." Cybill ran her hands over Storm's exposed breasts, teased the already taut nipples and ran her hands up and down Storm's body. Storm sat with her legs spread over Cybill's crotch. Storm leaned back to fully flaunt her naked body for Cybill, and Cybill enjoyed it as she grasped and squeezed a nipple.

Before Cybill knew what was happening, Storm tied her arms to the top bedpost and spread her legs to tie them to the opposing bottom posts.

"Now I've got you just where I want you." Storm looked at Cybill spread-eagled across the bed. She reached down and donned a large strap-on, which had only ever been used on her.

"Think you can take it?" Storm rubbed the tool across Cybill's mound. Without waiting for a response, Storm grabbed onto Cybill's hips and pushed the full length into Cybill's waiting body. It slid in to the hilt, before Storm pulled it out and shoved it back in.

Cybill could feel the tool slide in, filling her. She felt totally exposed and spread out. She couldn't move an inch as Storm pulled the dildo out and thrust it back in, out, then in again.

She was used to being on top, to being the one who used the dildo, not the one it was used on. But she enjoyed this variation.

She heard herself moan as Storm slowed the movement. She tried to arch it back in, but Storm played it over her swollen, wet clit.

"You want something?" she heard Storm say. She moaned her reply.

Suddenly, Storm was beating it in and out, in and out again. Her entire consciousness was focused between her legs as she was filled, then emptied. Her clit felt ready to explode as it cried for attention.

In the hotel room, Brett grabbed a strawberry off the nearby service, covered it with whipped cream and held it between her teeth. Allie grinned, stepped out of her heels and walked over to share the treat.

"I've been wanting to do this all night." Brett knelt in front of Allie and reached up her long legs to pull off her stockings, which were fastened with a garter belt, then unfastened her dress and let it slide to the ground. Allie wasn't wearing anything underneath. "Oh, God. Every single time I see your body, it takes my breath away."

Allie began to undress Brett. Brett stood, pulled Allie's leg over her hip and pulled her in tight, wrapping her arms around Allie, then they kissed.

Brett lay Allie on the bed and began to draw patterns across Allie's breasts with the whipped cream. Allie moaned as Brett licked it off, sliding her tongue across Allie's increasingly tense nipples, then playfully biting and pulling on them with her teeth.

Brett lay between Allie's legs and spread Allie's lips open with her fingers as Allie arched in anticipation. Brett wanted to take her, to make her come. Allie stretched her legs even further, as if trying to entice Brett to lick harder, faster. She threw her arms up to grab the headboard. Brett carefully ran her thumb up and down Allie's slick clit, then used both thumbs to rub her harder, pressing in on the wedge with both thumbs. She moved her hands back up to Allie's breasts, where she pinched the nipples while her tongue flicked up and down her clit, tasting Allie's sweet juices. Allie lay sprawled across the bed, with Brett's hands feeling every curve of her body.

Storm lay on top of Cybill and rode her hot cunt with the tremendous dildo. Cybill, ready to explode, could feel the softness of Storm's breasts against her as Storm rode her hard, brutally thrusting in before pulling out again. She was sitting on the edge, exposed, as her clit pulsated and her nipples ached.

Storm was sweating, and the wetness further enticed Cybill. Friction flew between their bodies, and Cybill could feel every inch of the tool as it was pulled out its entire length and then shoved back in until it felt like it was going to come out the top of her head.

Storm was vicious, using Cybill, and Cybill was loving it.

Allie felt Brett insert first one, then two, then three fingers, pulling them in then out, curving them up, all the while beating Allie's clit with her tongue.

Brett inserted her entire fist into Allie. Allie could not believe it, Brett had never done that to her before. She couldn't believe it fit, but it felt so good. She felt about to burst, with her clit pulsing in time with Brett's tongue. She arched her cunt into the air, as Brett twisted and turned the fist she had impaled Allie on.

Allie could feel the wave of sensation starting. She wrapped her legs around Brett's neck, and felt Brett lift her ass off the bed and into the air. Her stomach and ass tightened as the contractions began with Brett's fist, while her tongue pressed into her, brutally beating her swollen clit, focusing, beating it back and forth.

Allie tightened her legs around her neck and bucked.

"Brett! Brett!" Allie screamed, nearly tossing Brett off the bed.

* * * * *

"Oh God!" Cybill screamed, as the front door opened and the intruder headed directly for the bedroom.

Cybill and Storm looked up in shock as the bedroom door opened and they saw the intruder, but before they could move, the gun fired once, then twice.

PART TWO:
TILL DEATH DO US PART

Five years later

CHAPTER 15
Randi

"Rick DeSilva was buried today," Randi McMartin said, entering the office. "Both Brett Higgins and Franklin Lorenzini were present, each looking appropriately sorrowful."

She plopped her lanky frame in a chair and looked across the desk at Greg Morrow. Over the past five years Randi felt like she'd aged ten. Her always lean, athletic 5′6″ frame had gotten leaner, practically skinny; she'd noticed the laugh lines on her face became wrinkles and the gray in her dark brown hair became more pronounced. The change was most apparent, though, in her eyes: the dark pools had grown almost icy, and that scared her.

"I think there's going to be a war," he said with a frown as he dug through his desk for the rest of a doughnut.

The early summer sunlight streamed through the window, illuminating each speck of dust playing through the air of Morrow's small, cramped office. A variety of mugs, napkins, crumpled paper and fast food wrappers covered his desk, the wastebasket was overflowing, and folders and papers covered the floor in precarious stacks.

"I think Higgins did it," Randi said. Greg found the doughnut, stood and paced back and forth behind the desk while he quickly disposed of the rest of it.

"Randi, listen, it just doesn't make sense. DeSilva and Higgins were friends, and you don't just kill your boss so you can take over his operation."

"It's a gut feeling I have."

"But that's not the way these people operate."

"It makes perfect sense. She knocks him off, everyone else thinks it was an outside job, probably pulled by Jack O'Rourke, and she takes over his operations."

Greg sat down. He looked tired of the long hours, and Randi knew they'd had the same conversation several times in the past week. "I think you're giving Higgins a lot more, and a lot less, credit than she's due. She's different than a lot of these types — she's educated, talented and brave. She could have had DeSilva wrapped around her little finger if she wanted."

Randi looked out the window. She didn't like what she saw. Although construction crews had littered the city since Dennis Archer became mayor, fixing overpasses before they collapsed on traffic, filling in a few of the potholes created by Michigan's fickle climate, and replacing the burnt-out bulbs in streetlights in the more populated areas, and although Archer had instituted city-wide clean-up days, trying to inspire its denizens to fix up abandoned lots and gather litter from the streets, parks and walks, the city, deep down beneath its surface, was still the same. You had to get to these germs, these criminals, in order to really fix the problem, Randi thought. Getting it cleaner and in better repair helped, but more police were also needed to make it safer.

Thinking about safety brought her back to the conversation, back to the criminal at hand: Brett Higgins.

She wanted Higgins, had wanted her for five long years. One of her favorite fantasies was of pointing a gun at Brett as Brett kneeled before her, begging for her life, much as many people had probably done to Brett over the years. A part of Randi wanted witnesses to her revenge on that lowlife, but the more rational part knew that, if there were witnesses, she couldn't do what she wanted. That was one of the bad things about being a cop or a detective — you couldn't mete out the much deserved justice, you had to leave that to a jury, and between the juries and the judges, justice was rarely served.

She knew she shouldn't think this way, but couldn't help herself. All of these feelings had built up inside her and kept building each time she saw her parents' eyes when someone mentioned Danny, or when she entered Danny's room. In some ways it was an obsession, but Brett had also become a symbol to Randi of all that was wrong in and with the city. This obsession focused her anger so that she didn't do what a lot of other cops did — drink, beat their families, or beat up whoever looked vulnerable at the moment.

Regardless, she knew Brett was a criminal who deserved to be brought to justice, just like all the other criminals in the city. She smiled at the thought that the DeSilva operation just happened to be among the ones she and Morrow were assigned to watch.

Greg looked at Randi, shrugged and opened up the DeSilva file for the eightieth time this week. Both he and Randi knew the file's story by heart, as he had been compiling it for over five years now, the last two with Randi's help. Randi had been transferred, by her request, from homicide and into the special organized crime investigation squad just two years before.

Randi pushed her fingers through her hair. Greg had spent so much time tracking the DeSilva operations, he just couldn't see it anymore. Couldn't see Brett for the criminal she was. She watched Greg flip through the DeSilva file. He had it memorized, but obviously still hoped something might jump into his arms from its pages.

"Hold on," she said, flipping back a shot. "I've never seen this one before."

"It's always been here."

The photo was taken outside of the Ritz-Carlton hotel in Dearborn and showed a tuxedoed Brett leading a tall, blond woman from a taxi into the hotel.

"Who's she?"

"Allison Sullivan. She dated Brett for about six months about five years ago."

"Looks young."

"She was just seventeen when this was taken."

"So now Higgins is a cradle-robber, too."

"Good-looking girl, though."

"Yeah, but why're they all dressed up?"

"It was some sort of a prom night. The stupid thing about this picture is that it probably got your beloved Brett Higgins off of a murder charge."

Randi vaguely recalled having seen Sullivan around the time her brother was killed. She had never figured out why such an attractive, apparently nice girl was hooked up with a loser like Brett.

"Within an hour after this picture was taken, two women were killed across town. One was Allison's best friend, Cybill, and the other was Brett's other lover, Storm."

Greg seemed to feel a need to explain this, although Randi already knew it all. "She was a dancer at the Paradise," she said, to remind him of her vast knowledge of Brett Higgins.

"Yeah, the two women were in bed together when they were killed."

"They were both killed?"

Greg nodded. "We would've thought it was Brett in a jealous rage. Except that I can testify she spent the night in the hotel with Allison."

"So who did do it?" Randi asked, trying to remember.

"Probably one of Storm's fans. She had had some problems before and it appears Brett usually fixed them, except for this time. But, as we both know, once is all it takes."

Yeah, Brett usually "fixed" Storm's little problems . . . Just like she "fixed" Storm's supposed problem with Danny. "And Cybill was just in the wrong place at the wrong time," Randi said. Greg nodded. "So what happened with Allison and Brett?" She had been in such a rage at the time that she never noticed when Allison fell out of the picture.

"They broke up. Brett took Storm's death personally. She's never been quite the same."

"What about Allison?" Randi studied the picture. She knew that face from somewhere . . . Somewhere recent, more recent than the days when she had watched Brett after her brother's murder.

"She's been out of the picture for about five years now. She was just graduating high school when they broke up and offhand that's all I know about her. Once she was out of the picture, there was no need to continue keeping track of her."

Randi studied the photo. Even from a distance, the two women looked very much in love. Brett looked at Allison with total devotion. But, Randi reminded herself, Brett had another lover on the side. She was slime, born slime, raised slime, and would die slime. And Randi would do everything in her power to make sure that happened as soon as possible. But where did she know Allison from?

"Do you have any other pictures of Sullivan?" Randi asked Greg.

CHAPTER 16
Allie

Allie wiped her eyes and already chapped nose and headed for her car. She tried to avoid the annoying swarm of sympathetic relatives. She shrugged away from the few who tried to corner her in the open cemetery, not needing or wanting their so-called help or sympathy.

"Oh, Allie, are you okay?" said nosy Aunt Gertrude, pushing her glasses up on her nose. Another blue-haired old lady stood next to her, a woman Allie knew she should recognize but didn't.

"Yeah, I just need to get some sleep," Allie replied, hurrying off. She didn't really care what the relatives had to say about her. She just wanted to get home and into a nice, hot bath. She climbed into her car and drove.

The house was empty now. She carefully locked the door behind her, sat in her father's great armchair and cried. She cried for her father and for her mother, too, who was gone just six months now. But, most of all, she cried for herself and how truly alone she was.

She had taken the past week off work in order to put his things in order and to prepare for the funeral. As expected, she was his sole heir. She now owned the house, for which there were only a few payments left, his car, and everything else he had collected in his almost seventy years on this planet, as well as his large insurance policy.

She walked into her room and looked at her uniform. She had graduated from college on time and gone on to the police academy. She was now a Southfield police officer. Her parents had always questioned her desire to become a cop, even though it was clearly in the Sullivan blood. Now, though, this uniform was her lifeline, her reason to keep going.

When Cybill was killed, it had strengthened her resolve to become a police officer, especially when Cybill's murderer was never found; now, however, with her mother gone of cancer just six months and her father recently dead from a heart attack, it was all she really had left.

Her parents had been there for her when Cybill

died, and then when she and Brett broke up. They had been their always kind, understanding selves. Now they were gone and she was more alone than she had ever been before in her life.

She wandered about the house, looking at old family pictures, fingering the dusty frames and promising herself to do the spring cleaning soon. After Mom died, Dad had just about lost his will to live. Allie was probably the only reason he did anything during these past six months, but she wasn't enough. She could only hope to ever find the love that they had shared for almost forty years.

She probably could've engaged the help of some of her relatives, like Aunt Gertrude, to help her clean, but the thought of those people digging through her parents' possessions seemed somehow sacrilegious. She walked into her room and lay on the bed. She stared at the ceiling and knew she couldn't sleep, no matter how much she needed to.

The phone rang. She must've dozed off. When she answered the phone, a disguised voice said, "The poor little kitten's all alone now," and hung up.

Allie looked at the phone and wondered what to do. She picked up pen and paper and wrote down the exact time and words used. She stared at the paper, musing over the words, and realized very few people knew her father had called her his little kitten. When she tossed the tablet back on the desk, an old picture slipped from its spot in a crack. Allie stopped and looked at it.

Brett was particularly handsome in her black tuxedo and Allie shivered, remembering Brett's arm around her while they posed for her parents, and then, Brett's lips on hers that night . . .

The next morning, Allie and Brett were taking a shower together, the hot water warming their already over-heated bodies, when Brett's pager went off. Brett donned a bathrobe and returned the call. She said a few words into the phone, then dropped it on the floor. Allie saw this from the bathroom. She rushed over to Brett and all Brett would say was "Oh my God."

That was the only time Allie had ever seen Brett cry.

Of course, it didn't take long for Allie to find out that Cybill was gone, too. And it wasn't long after that that Brett admitted to Allie that she and Storm had been lovers. All in one fell blow, Allie lost both her lover and her best friend. Brett blamed herself for not protecting Storm and felt guilty because she had supposedly dumped Storm just that day, and Allie blamed Brett for introducing Cybill to Storm, because they all figured it was one of Storm's johns who did them in.

All that seemed like nothing now, although at the time Allie had thought her world was at an end. Now she knew what rock bottom was. When all she had left was her job, she knew it couldn't get any worse. There really was no one left for her to lose . . .

She gazed at the smile on Brett's face, the smile that was no more. She only occasionally heard of Brett, but mostly she saw her on TV or in the newspapers denying something, and she was never smiling, and that same thing was still there in her dark eyes. She could no longer tell what color they were.

Through sources at work, Allie learned that DeSilva had expanded his operations and was trying to take over turf from other players in the high-stakes lottery of crime.

Five years ago Allie would never have expected Brett to end up this way. From what she could tell, Brett was cold and cruel, calculating and exact, when she had always seemed vivacious and alive, living just for the next chance. Her eyes used to be filled with laughter and love; now they seemed like dark orbs that revealed nothing.

CHAPTER 17
Brett

"I don't care what you have to do, do it," Brett barked at Frankie. "Find out who did it, and let me know. Killing is too good for him . . . I want in on it, though." The look in Frankie's eyes said that he knew she meant business.

They had just returned from Rick's funeral and were seated in Brett's officc, talking game plans.

Rick's will was to be read in a few hours, but they already knew he had left everything to the two of them.

When the businesses grew, they moved the magazines and other items into a warehouse and now the space above the theater was reserved solely for Brett, Frankie and Rick's offices. No longer did employees rush about — now the place was secure.

Brett had deliberately chosen the windowless office and furnished it with deep burgundy carpeting and polished wood furniture — a comfortable sofa, coffee table, three sets of bookshelves and a large oak desk. Floor lamps provided the lighting the desk lamp could not, and a few Ansel Adams prints decorated the walls. Brett enjoyed the elegant simplicity the black and white photography conveyed; she loved the way Adams could so capture moments of tempestuous fury or graceful calm.

Brett's office was quite a contrast to the glossy metal of Rick's office and the near shambles of Frankie's office. Frankie liked the bareness of his office, especially because the few times he had to conduct business there it helped his image of a rough-cut no-nonsense sort of fellow.

Brett paced the floor, lost in thought and her eyes wandered up to the bookshelf on which, at opposing ends, she had situated pictures of Allie and Storm. Her mind flew back to those days of happiness and decisions, and to the days of anguish that concluded that phase of her life. A tear crept into her eye for the women she had loved and the person she had been.

These days she truly knew the meaning of the phrase *Constant Craving* — not a day went by that she didn't think of Allie and all she had lost.

"Why don't you give her a call?" Frankie asked.

"No. I can't." He always seemed to know what she was thinking.

"You still love her, don't ya?"

"Yeah, but I guess I'm afraid she wouldn't love me."

"Aren't ya even curious what happened to her?"

"Yeah, but my mind prefers to remember her as she was, and as we were together. She wouldn't fit into my life anymore."

"I guess we only got each other," Frankie said, putting an arm companionably around Brett's shoulders.

"I guess you're right."

Rick, Brett and Frankie had grown the businesses over the past few years. Rick oversaw all activities and created a few new ones, while Brett was, basically, the business/marketing/advertising manager, and Frankie, well, Frankie was Frankie, taking care of things that fell outside of Rick's and Brett's jurisdictions, which ended up mostly as "security."

Brett and Frankie both knew each other's talents and shortcomings, so working as a team would leave no problems. As for what were normally Rick's activities, they would divide those, except the ones that would require them both. Brett had learned that no matter how much she worked out, she was not a man, and the only way to deal in some of the paths she had to was either with a bodyguard or a very large gun. Preferably an Uzi. No matter what her questionably feminist leanings were, too much in this world was brawn as opposed to brain. Although she could easily outwit them, she couldn't do that unless they'd listen to her.

She knew Frankie often had good ideas and contacts, but he also had a tendency to underestimate his own potential. She knew he was an eager learner and wanted to know more about running the business, because he couldn't go on being a strong arm all his life. Not unless he planned on it ending very soon.

"Don't worry, we'll get the motherfucker," Frankie said as they left the office.

"Hey, I thought you were taking me out to dinner between shows," Kirsten said, walking up behind Brett. She had come up the stairs, the door at the bottom of which they had accidentally left unlocked.

"Uh, yeah, okay," Brett said quickly looking at her watch, then tightening her tie back up. "Lemme just grab my jacket."

Frankie stood coolly leaning against a wall with his arms crossed, giving Kirsten the evil eye. Kirsten looked at him as Brett grabbed her jacket from her office and locked up behind her.

"Y'know I'll help you move your stuff when you move into Rick's office," Kirsten said loudly, obviously for the benefit of both Frankie and Brett. Frankie went to his office, supposedly to make a few phone calls. Kirsten and Frankie had never gotten along — he didn't like, nor trust, Kirsten.

He and Brett had talked about Kirsten quite a bit. Brett tried to assuage his feelings by telling him she was just using Kirsten, that they were just fuck-buddies, but he insisted that Kirsten had a fatal attraction for Brett. He claimed she knew too much about the business for his liking. Brett told him Kirsten would never turn against her in that way, but he just wasn't too sure what Kirsten's limits and scruples were, if she had any.

The only thing they could agree about was that they both liked the money she made them. The men loved her, flocking down from the suburbs to see her the one week a month she danced.

"I do wish you'd get rid of those pictures when you move, though," Kirsten said to Brett, referring to the photographs of Storm and Allie.

"I don't care. They're staying."

"As far as you're concerned, they might as well both be dead."

"That doesn't matter."

"You can't spend your life crying over spilt blood."

"No, but I can remember." Brett knew she was cold and cruel and she enjoyed it.

CHAPTER 18
Plots and Plans

Randi entered the dimly lit bar. A cloud of smoke hovered near the ceiling and Randi knew that, as the night progressed, the cloud would slowly grow until it enveloped the entire bar as a cancerous leech grows to take over and kill the host organism.

She usually didn't go to the bars because she didn't like the loud music, the drunken recklessness, the sleazy come-ons and the omnipresent smoke cloud, but she had been here every night this past week searching for Allison Sullivan. Fortunately, in Detroit, there really weren't too many lesbian bars — in fact, it was mostly just the Railroad Crossing, a dance bar, and Sugarbaker's, a sports bar.

It had taken her several hours of staring at the photos and notes on Sullivan before she realized where she had seen the elusive dyke before: at the Railroad Crossing, which was, interestingly enough, located on Eight Mile between Mound and Van Dyke. Of course it made perfect sense for a twenty-three-year-old lesbian to hang around a lesbian bar. Randi briefly toyed with the idea of merely approaching Allison at home or work, but laid aside that idea in favor of a less business-like approach of initially befriending her and then asking for her cooperation in the prosecution of Brett Higgins.

Greg Morrow didn't like the plan. He figured there was a reason Sullivan and Higgins had split up and that this animosity was mirrored by the fact that there were no records of any communication between the two for five years. Of course, Randi remembered with a grin, he had no idea of the ties between lesbians and their exes, and she really hadn't felt like educating him on the matter. Plus, there was something there, at least to Randi. It just didn't make sense to her that the two women lived so near each other but never spoke or visited. Randi figured she knew Brett well enough at this point to be able to safely wager she wouldn't turn down any proposition the enigmatic Allison made.

Randi grinned again when she thought of Allison. There was something almost mystical about the slender blond who had lost so much in the past few years. A woman who could live through that, have enough balls to become a Southfield cop and look like that — well, that was just the sort of woman Randi definitely wanted to associate with.

Randi went to the bar, ordered a beer, then watched several minutes of an intense pool game, certain it was another wasted evening. She thought about lining up her quarters at one of the tables, but opted for a walk through the crowded bar instead. She wandered past the dance floor, carefully examining all the women there, although she had a feeling Allison — or would she go by "Allie"? — wasn't there. She went outside to the patio for a welcome breath of fresh air and studied the stars up above.

She finished her beer and headed to the door to leave, but noticed a familiar mane of blond hair across the crowd, heading toward the dance floor. She quickly weaved through the crowd in pursuit.

Allie stopped to talk with someone Randi didn't recognize. The woman hugged Allie. Randi frowned, grabbed a waitress, asked that a beer be sent to Allie and watched as the waitress delivered the beer. Allie eyed Randi, took the beer, and nodded in Randi's direction as a silent thanks. Her companion leaned over and whispered something to her. Allie laughed.

Randi walked up behind Allie and put her hand on her shoulder. Allie turned slightly and looked up at her. "You remind me of someone I once knew." Randi pulled out a chair and sat down.

Allie raised an eyebrow. "Have a seat."

"I will."

"Give me a call this week, maybe we can do dinner," the other woman said, getting up to leave.

"That sounds like fun," Allie replied. Randi noticed the woman had a smirk on her face. Allie turned to face Randi. "Thanks for the brew."

There was something about her short sentences, directness and frankness that Randi found compelling. Not to mention the fact that not a single one of the photographs could hold a light to the true blue, slightly more mature version of the woman.

"So is it a good person, or a bad person," Randi said, "that I remind you of?"

"A little of both," Allie replied, a faraway look in her eyes as she seemed to stare at a point just above Randi's right shoulder.

"Well, why don't we try for only the good?"

"But bad is so much more fun."

"My name's Randi." Randi introduced herself, ignoring the dare, and asked, "Was that your girlfriend?"

"Her? No, just a friend." Allie took a sip of her beer.

"So who is this half bad/half good person I remind you of?"

"Oh, um, an ex-girlfriend."

"Well, she couldn't have been that good if she's your ex." Randi tried to avoid frowning at the idea of being compared to Brett. Randi couldn't figure what someone like Allie had ever seen in Brett Higgins. Allie seemed to be very honest and forthright, and a little gentle and tender around the edges. Although she seemed to be holding back, afraid to say too much too soon, Allie seemed like just the sort of woman Randi had been looking for. Randi was a bit disturbed that Allie still seemed to be taken by Brett, because not only could she not understand what she saw in Brett in the first place, but also because that made it seem more unlikely that Allie would have any power over Brett. It must have been Brett Randi thought, who had called off the relationship. Randi looked up at Allie and couldn't help smiling. She decided that the time spent in meeting this woman was not wasted.

"She was good, she was bad, and a lot of shit happened," Allie said, her eyes still glazed.

"Hey . . ." Randi put a hand on Allie's cheek and tilted Allie's face to meet her eyes. "Shit happens everywhere, all the time. You just have to learn to cope with it."

Allie looked into Randi's eyes, then put her hand on Randi's.

"I know. It's just that sometimes it all seems like too much," she said.

"Allie, the music's gettin' kinda loud, and the smoke is descending. Do you want to go someplace else to talk?" Randi all but yelled, trying to be heard over the particularly loud dance number. Bodies were writhing all over the dance floor.

"That would be nice."

The Backstage burned down in 1993, leaving only a charred building and destroyed artifacts to attest that it once was. Irreplaceable theatrical memorabilia had been lost in the fire --- of course, the fire department's presence at the burning had been a joke, they wasted far too much time in trying to put it out, obviously appreciating that it was a gay establishment whose presence in Detroit was flying into the night sky as flames and smoke. It was only amazing that they hadn't brought marshmallows with them to the fire that night.

Backstage finally reopened in Royal Oak, but Allie didn't think it'd last very long, not with such competition as Pronto! 608, a gay restaurant where the food was actually good, located just across the street in downtown Royal Oak, which was becoming a very gay place indeed.

"So who was this woman who done you wrong?" Randi said with a grin as they were seated at a table in the back of Pronto! 608.

"It wasn't really that she did me wrong, it was more the fault of circumstances, and I was young, and she took things very hard."

When the waitress first pointed Randi out, Allie had felt her heart quicken until she realized it was not Brett. Randi was a bit shorter than Brett and her hair was brown, not black, although it was styled similarly, albeit half the dykes in town wore their hair in that style. Allie thought it was the attitude and the clothes Randi wore that reminded her of Brett. Randi's black jeans, black boots and silk shirt were exactly the sort of thing Brett would've chosen. She didn't exactly think of Brett daily, but she hadn't forgotten her. Time may heal all wounds, but it was taking much longer than Allie ever expected to get over Brett.

Allie looked up and into Randi's eyes. She really hadn't dated much since Brett. There had been a few women, but none of them ever seemed to match up to Brett, or came close to being her soulmate. There was something about Randi she liked, something in her eyes, something familiar about her. She seemed to want to be the strong one, and Allie was growing tired of being strong.

"You're a very understanding person," Randi said, forcing Allie back into the present.

"Sometimes that's the worst sort of person to be." It was as if this woman was placed here at this moment in time to help her.

They ordered their drinks and talked. Allie found Randi easy to talk with, and found herself saying much more than she normally would on a first date. It was almost an outpouring produced from spending too much time alone. Since her father had died, she really hadn't felt like socializing, but at the urging of a few friends, she decided to go out tonight instead of stewing in the muddle of her own mind.

Allie refused a third drink, so Randi paid their bill and walked her out to her car.

"Well, Allie," Randi began. There was warmth in her voice. "It was real nice talking with you."

Allie shrugged and gave her a shy smile. "Thanks for listening."

"I'd really like to see you again."

"I'd like that, too." She felt the warm breeze play gently with her hair. Moonlight both accented and shadowed Randi's features.

"Good." Randi smiled at her, then paused as if she were thinking of something else. "Ah, I guess I need your phone number."

Allie grinned. "That might help." She pulled out a pen and paper and jotted it down. When she handed it to Randi, their fingers lingered, touching briefly, before Randi pocketed the number and Allie let her hand fall back to her side. Allie looked down, uncertain what to say. Suddenly, Randi leaned forward and brushed her lips against Allie's. Allie started to respond but pulled away, shyness overcoming her. "I've got to go. Give me a call, okay?"

CHAPTER 19
Kirsten

As Kirsten slipped her bra off, the music coursed through her body like an electrical current. Her nipples became hard and extended — touched both by the cool breeze from the air conditioning and the gaze from the fifty or so men seated in the auditorium. The pounding rhythm coursed through the building. She could feel it coming into her through the floors, vibrating off the walls; she could see it in the eyes of the men.

She danced, letting the music possess her and take her over, moving her hands down over her hips and then back up to tease her nipples. She glanced out over the audience, making eye contact with one of her regulars, giving him a sly, seductive smile that he would think was meant only for him. The near chanting backbeat rhythm of Prince, his dirty, explicit lyrics, rang throughout the place.

She knew that three years ago Brett had given her this job in order to degrade her. At that point, she had hoped to be Brett's next Storm, to be taken under Brett's wing and coddled. That didn't happen. But Kirsten learned to love her job regardless. She liked the power she had over these men, these animals. She liked knowing she could, and would, turn them on, make them hard and ready.

She had chosen the stage name Venus. All the dancers used stage names, not only to protect their true identities, but also to further arouse the men's imaginations. She thought Venus particularly apropos for her; she felt like a goddess everytime she stepped onstage — the goddess of sexual love and beauty.

Not only did she enjoy dancing, she made very good money at it, occasionally more than $5,000 per week. She could live fairly comfortably on what she made and spend the other three weeks of the month doing whatever she wanted, which at the moment was college. She had begun taking classes to better herself like Storm had, but Brett wasn't buying, so when she got her degree, she'd have to determine what to do next. All she knew was she didn't want to give up working at the theater. She liked it too much.

She danced naked on the stage, flaunting her

body and the possibilities it held. She saw the men squirm in their seats, some opening their pants to jerk themselves off. She heard them groan and she leaned over to fully reveal the secrets held between her legs. She spread her lips and dipped her fingers into the juices, which she ran over her tits while she gyrated her hips in rhythm to the music, sliding into a hip-jerk that left nothing to the imagination.

Her music was always much more direct and pounding than Storm's had been. Kirsten thought Storm's ethereal, mood music too subtle, too wishy-washy. She preferred the directness of Prince's lyrics, the lyrics of now, the lyrics of sex and sweat and fucking. She liked hard beats, direct music, music she could feel throughout her entire body. She liked it loud so there was no mistaking her intent. She wanted it to overwhelm.

She looked into the audience and spotted one man hurriedly puffing on a cigarette, wearing a post-sex expression on his face, intently watching her every move. She smiled down on him from her perch on top of the stage. The second song was nearing its end, so she strutted across the stage to retrieve her g-string and turn down the lights so that the men she was not dancing for could watch the movie. She almost hated putting on the g-string, covering up any part of her nakedness, which she reveled in.

She pitied these men who came to her hoping that she could fulfill some need their lives had not met. It wasn't a good pity. They were inferior beings, willing to give her whatever she requested just to be able to touch her, to smell her, to be with her. She had them tied around her little finger and they were as loyal as the mangy mutts some people save from the pound. They required very little of her in return, thankful for anything she would stoop to giving them.

Kirsten tossed her long auburn hair back across her shoulders and entered the audience, selecting the first to buy a lap dance from her. The music was turned down lower, but not too low. She still liked to feel the beat pulse through her veins like the sweetest narcotic of all.

She rubbed her body against one man and allowed him to feel her hips. It disturbed her that Brett wouldn't throw those old pictures in the trash where they belonged, especially not after all she, Kirsten, had done for Brett and her career. She was going to win her over, once and for all. The only roadblock she saw standing in her way was Allie, for even though Allie was no longer in Brett's life, she was in her mind, and Kirsten knew this. Whenever Brett became extremely passionate, Kirsten knew she wasn't thinking about her, but about Storm or Allie.

The man ran his hands over her breasts, pausing on her nipples. This was illegal, but it felt good, so Kirsten let him do it.

Allie. A loose piece in the picture. She'd take care of that. When she saw how both Brett and Allie reacted to the deaths of Cybill and Storm, she knew which woman she wanted. There was something wild, animal, brutal in Brett's behavior, whereas Allie simply lost some small part of herself. Each time Allie suffered a loss, she lost some bit, so that she was no longer a complete woman. Kirsten wanted a whole woman. Right now she had Brett in her bed. That was a start. Brett would soon be entirely hers.

The man began to push the thin strip of the g-string to the side, trying to get his fingers inside her.

Kirsten pushed him aside as she would any other insect and went on to the next customer.

She looked up and smiled. In the next row back in the auditorium, a well-dressed man waved a hundred-dollar bill at her. Out of courtesy to her regular, well-paying customer she ignored the nearer clients who only proffered twenties.

This man had, at first, mystified her — his face and eyes said he wanted to touch her, but then he said he didn't want a lap dance. It was only after several months at the Paradise that Kirsten discovered she was wearing too much perfume, as most of the dancers did. The well-off married men from the suburbs didn't like that because it was the one odor they couldn't excuse to their wives as part of an intense boardroom meeting.

She smiled at the man, who nodded as she took the proffered bill. "Hi there," she intoned softly, in her deepest, sexiest voice. "What can I do for you today?" He smiled as she put her legs on the arms of the chair, and he ran his hands up her thighs, clearly en- joying the softness that coated the muscles. She leaned forward to let him enjoy her breasts, even as the beat played on, with the sensual lyrics continuing.

CHAPTER 20
When We Meet Again

It happened on the fifth date. Randi was getting worried because she knew Frankie was working the town over trying to get to the bottom of the Rick matter. She suspected Brett did it, and therefore a lot of people were going to be needlessly hurt and/or killed before anything was resolved. Plus, she had been waiting a long time to get Brett, and now she was so close she could practically see her spilled blood.

Randi enjoyed Allie's company, as well as her looks and her body, but knew she had to lay it out in the open before things got too serious. They had slept together, but no commitments had yet been made.

The first time she was in Allie's bedroom, she noticed the picture of Brett, but still waited a few days before asking about it.

"That's Brett," Allie said.

"The infamous ex?" Randi feigned surprise.

"Yeah. Do you want anything to eat before you go?"

"No thanks." Pause. It was obvious Allie wouldn't continue the conversation of her own free will. "Why do you still have her picture around?"

"What's any picture for, Randi? To help you remember the important times in your life. The people you once loved."

"Allie, there's something you need to know . . ." Randi took a deep breath. Allie listened quietly, patiently, while Randi explained the reason she had wanted to meet Allie, and the plan she had to capture Brett and bring her to justice. She explained that if Allie agreed, Detroit might be able to borrow her from Southfield as an intra-force criminal activities liaison, and then Allie would be, at least temporarily, able to work in a promoted spot as a detective, which would look very good on her record. She expected Allie to rant and rave and hate her for using her, but Allie surprised her.

"Obviously, you didn't need to go to bed with me to ask me this."

"No, I didn't. That was Randi the person, not Randi the cop."

"And this is all right with your chief?"

"Actually, up to this point, only my partner has even an inkling what's up. But because you're a cop in Southfield, I don't think there'd be any problem using you as bait."

"Bait?"

"I think she'd open up to you."

"What makes you think she gives a shit about me?"

"Because it doesn't look like she's had a real relationship since you, and because of the way it appears you two broke up . . ."

"That was a bad time for both of us."

"It's evident you still have feelings for her."

"Yeah, but that was years ago."

"She's not the same woman anymore, Allie. In fact, I think she killed Rick DeSilva."

"He was her friend, why would she do that?"

"Only way to get a promotion in that business."

"Are you sure we're talking about the same Brett Higgins?"

Randi left shortly after that, leaving Allie to think over her proposition. She made it perfectly clear that regardless of Allie's decision on this, she still wanted to date her.

Allie didn't think Brett could have done all the things Randi said she did, but she also realized that Randi wouldn't give up regardless of her answer. Therefore, she reasoned, she should do it, because that was the only way she could find out for certain who the new Brett Higgins was. Plus, the promotion, even if temporary, was tempting. She didn't need the money, but the challenge of being a detective was compelling.

She picked up the picture and looked at Brett's smiling eyes. The only remaining question then was whether or not Brett would welcome her back into her life.

Allie fell asleep holding Brett's picture in her arms.

It took very little to convince Greg Morrow of Allie's capabilities of becoming an inside agent. He wasn't sure one way or the other how Brett would react to Allie, whether or not she would want her back in her life, but Randi seemed certain she would. As soon as both the departments were satisfied, Randi and Greg set to work on preparing Allie for her assignment.

Allie would pose as the manager of a small boutique in Troy that Randi's cousin owned. Randi chose that cover because she knew she could trust Sally not to mess up. Allie had given up on her dreams of becoming an officer when Cybill's killer was not discovered. Or that was what Brett was to believe.

Randi and Greg decided it would be in Allie's best interests to know as much as possible about the woman she was dealing with, so they set about carefully going over the files with Allie. They wanted her prepared so she would not be caught blindsided.

Then, one night over dinner, Randi was quizzing Allie on the "facts" of her life when she decided to arm her with one last other thing. "It seems like a lot of people around Brett end up either dead or in the hospital."

"What do you mean?" Allie asked in disbelief. Randi merely looked back at her. "And you think she's doing it herself?"

"If not her, then she's giving the orders."

"Can you prove it?"

"It's just an assumption at the moment, that's why we need you."

"And you think she's gonna confess it all just like that," Allie snapped her fingers.

"No. But I want you to watch yourself."

"Yes, ma'am," Allie sarcastically replied, obviously still not believing Brett could change that much. But Randi didn't really think she had changed at all, just hidden much of herself from Allie while they dated.

"I'm serious, Allie, Brett Higgins is a dangerous woman, there's no telling what she might do next."

"I'm in," Allie said with a steel glint in her eyes. Randi smiled at her, although she never had a doubt.

CHAPTER 21
Out of the Blue

Allie drove by the House of Kinsey. She knew Brett no longer spent much time there, but she spent more time there than at any of the other stores. It was also the place Brett would be least suspicious of Allie walking into one day. It would be much more difficult to explain Allie's presence at the Paradise Theater, but she could always special-order a book from the House.

Allie had talked herself into taking this assignment mostly because of what it would do for her career, or so she had convinced herself, but the thought of ridding herself of Brett once and for all lurked in her mind. Allie really didn't believe a word Randi had said about Brett. Of course, there was the day Brett pulled a gun on some punks at her school . . . She could take the easy road and drop this case right now, but . . .

Allie parked across the divided highway, across the street from the store, and picked up her radio to inform Randi as to her position. Randi was down the street, near the theater, watching for Brett. Allie didn't see Brett's black Aurora anywhere in sight. Randi's mission was to try to keep an eye on Brett, but it was a low priority. It was more important that Allie not be noticed. The last thing they needed was for Brett to know something was going down. Although Greg and Randi had kept Brett under close surveillance since Rick's death, they had set it back to next-to-nothing while they prepared Allie for her mission. They knew that if Allie walked in from nowhere when Brett knew she was being followed, they'd never convince her it was an accident.

"I'm in place," Allie said into the transmitter.

"Good. She's upstairs right now."

"And day two's just beginning," Allie said, leaning back in her seat with a book. They figured it may take a couple of weeks to get Allie and Brett together naturally and Allie was not looking forward to spending that time doing something next to nothing.

"She's getting in her car," came the crackled voice over the speaker.

"Which way's she heading?"

"Out to Woodward. I'll keep you posted. She's by

herself." A few moments later Randi's voice came back. "She's heading north."

Allie sat up and looked toward the road. She could barely see Brett through the Aurora's slightly tinted windows, but she knew her and she knew the car. She moved lower in her seat as Brett parked by the House of Kinsey. When Brett got out of her car Randi's car went past.

"I'm going in," Allie said into the radio before hiding it under the seat. She glanced at her watch. It was 12:30. The House of Kinsey had just opened and she could say she was on lunch. Perfect.

Brett entered the store, coming for the deposits of the past several nights and in order to ask the on-duty clerk to become the manager.

Michelle looked up from the book she was reading and gave Brett a warm smile. "Heya."

"Heya yourself," Brett replied, unable to stop the smile that came to her lips. "How's things goin'?"

"Pretty good. I think you'll be happy," Michelle said.

Michelle was Brett's second in command here. Brett was grateful to her for that, especially because so many of the establishments lacked people with the sight, knowledge and ambition to manage them.

"Have a seat, I need to talk to you about something." Brett sat at the little table they had situated for people to read at.

"Can I get you some coffee first?"

"That would be wonderful."

"You take it 'of color,' correct?"

"Yeah," Brett smiled at Michelle's PC humor. Michelle went to get the coffee, and Brett allowed her eyes to wander down Michelle's slim figure and long dark hair. Michelle suddenly turned and caught Brett staring.

"Is something the matter?"

"No."

Michelle brought the coffee over and handed it to Brett, their fingers lightly brushing in the process. Brett looked up and into Michelle's deep brown eyes. She had never before noticed the softness of her skin, the caring in her eyes. She took a sip of the hot liquid.

"Mmmm . . . good."

"Thanks." A faint blush touched Michelle's cheeks. "It's my own blend."

If Brett didn't know better, she'd think Michelle was flirting with her. If she didn't know better . . . Suddenly she longed for Allie like she hadn't for a while — a month at least. She remembered the days when she used to date several women simultaneously. She had only touched Kirsten for over two years now — and she didn't even love Kirsten, or have any strong feelings for her.

"Are you all right?" Michelle reached across the table and brushed Brett's hand.

"Yeah, yeah, just thinking about an old friend."

"Rick?"

Brett looked down at their hands, and Michelle began to withdraw hers, but Brett took it and held it for a moment before letting it go.

"Michelle . . ." Her eyes once again met Michelle's.

The front door chime rang as a customer entered.

Brett looked up and Michelle jumped to her feet: supersales in action.

"Can I help you?" Michelle asked courteously.

Brett's heart skipped a beat. Allie, about to speak, smiled at Michelle, then noticed Brett. Their gazes locked into each other's. Brett couldn't believe Allie had become even more beautiful with maturity. The five years passed in a heartbeat.

"Hi," finally escaped from Allie's lips. Lips that had always been so soft.

"Is something the matter?" Michelle asked, glancing between Allie and Brett.

"Allie," was all Brett could manage.

"You look good," she said.

"You, too."

Michelle backed away from the two. Brett figured Michelle had been in her office enough to recognize Allie from her picture.

"I came here, uh, looking for a book," Allie finally stammered.

"Which one?" Brett didn't take her eyes off Allie, afraid that if she did Allie would disappear in a puff, only to have been a visitation from an overworked mind.

"*The Well of Loneliness.*"

"Oh, I don't usually stock that," Michelle said regretfully.

"Why not?" Brett asked, turning to her with genuine curiosity, glad for something else to think about.

"Have you ever read it?"

"No, but isn't it a classic?"

"I heard it was really depressing," Allie said.

"It is!" Michelle replied.

"Sounds like just the sort of thing I'd like to cuddle up with on a hot summer's night." Brett imagined herself cuddling with Allie.

"Would you like me to order it?" Michelle offered.

"That'd be great."

"Have you had lunch?" Brett took a step closer to Allie.

"Um, no, I haven't." Allie looked at her watch.

"Do you have somewhere to be?"

"I'm on lunch."

"Well, then, we'd better hurry." Brett brushed her hair back with her hand. "We can finish our talk later, Michelle."

Allie smiled at Brett and followed her through the door. "You drive."

Pronto's was fairly busy when they arrived, but Brett was a regular so she and Allie were quickly seated. After they ordered, Brett looked up into Allie's unbelievably deep blue eyes, lost her thought and sighed instead.

When Allie shot her a questioning look, Brett said, "So, what've you been up to?"

"A little of this and a lot of that."

"Did you finish college?"

"I . . . I changed my mind and decided I couldn't get into criminal justice. I couldn't become a cop."

"Oh really? What made you decide that?"

"Mostly Cybill and Storm."

Brett saw a cloud pass over Allie's face and reached across the table to take her hand. The feel of Allie's hand shocked Brett with its warmth, softness and gentleness. Brett was aware that she took Allie by surprise with the gesture, but she felt swept up by Allie's sadness. "I understand."

"That they never found out who did it and I'm not sure they really even tried."

Brett was afraid to bring up subjects best left alone. The waiter brought their drinks and she began to toy with the beer label. "So what are you up to now?"

"I'm managing a small boutique out in Troy."

"Oh, that must be interesting."

"Not really. But I'm hoping to go back for my bachelor's degree soon."

"Good for you."

There was an awkward silence. "So how's Rick doin'?"

"Not very well, I'm afraid."

"Why? What's the matter?"

"Someone killed him."

"How? Why?"

"Shot 'im and that's what I want to know."

"So what's up with the House and the Paradise and all that?"

"Rick left it all to Frankie and me — you remember Frankie, don't you?"

"Yeah, I do." Allie wiped some of the watery sweat off her glass. She looked up at Brett. "Do the police have any suspects?"

"You know the cops — the easiest answer must be the right one. But this is hardly a subject of small talk . . . So, you still living with your folks?"

"Um, I, they . . ."

"What's the matter, hon?" Brett sensed something was wrong.

"They're dead."

"Oh, my God. Allie." Brett reached across the table and held Allie's hands. "What happened?" Allie turned away from Brett and pulled her hands back into her lap.

"I . . . I don't want to talk about it."

Brett came to sit next to Allie. "What happened?" she asked again, pulling Allie into her arms. Allie began to cry. "Was it a car accident?"

Allie shook her head. "No, nothing so dramatic. Mom died of cancer and Dad died of a heart attack six months later."

"Shit. Oh, Allie, I'm so sorry." The waiter approached with their food, and pulled back nervously when he saw Allie wipe her eyes.

"This drink was really bad," Brett said without a hint of a smirk. "Why don't you bring us both a scotch." She turned back to Allie as the waiter scurried off. They were sitting thigh to thigh and she placed her hand along Allie's cheek, lifting Allie's head till their eyes met. "Let's get this wrapped and take it back to my office, where we can talk."

Allie protested about needing to get back to work, but Brett talked her into calling her clerk. When Allie got off the phone, Brett was waiting with a paper bag in hand. She led Allie to the car, and she drove to the theater. When they went upstairs, Frankie's door was closed, although loud voices could be heard from behind it.

"You've redecorated," Allie said as soon as they were in Brett's office.

"Yeah, we got too big, so we had to do some moving. The distribution center is located in a warehouse down on Woodward. We just handle all the management crap up here now."

Allie surveyed the office, glancing at the marketing and management books on the shelves. She stopped when she met her own smiling face. "You've done a nice job in here," she said suddenly, staring at her picture.

"Yeah, but I'll probably move to Rick's office soon. It's bigger and has a view."

"That's a good thing?"

"Ah, it just lets you see what the day's like. And around here, you get to see almost as much action as the latest Stallone flick."

"Business is good, I take it." Allie sat next to Brett on the sofa and took the Styrofoam container of food Brett had laid out. She had ordered Pronto's incredible chicken pot pie.

"Sex sells. Laws of supply and demand — they demand it, we sell it. Bingo. A match made in fucking heaven."

"You don't sound happy about it."

"Sometimes it gets me down. I see so much of the depravity in human nature. Mostly with the males of the species. I feel isolated in here. Sometimes it's a good isolation, sometimes not."

"Why don't you get out of it, then?"

"The pay's too damn good. Plus, what else would I do?"

"You've got a degree . . ."

"And that doesn't mean anything — as you'll soon learn. And I can't exactly list this place on my resumé. It can be fun, sometimes, though. Trying to figure out how to get people to come to my shops, instead of somewhere else. Of course, I get 'em either way because of the distribution chain."

"But . . ."

"Listen, we didn't come here to discuss business. At least, I hope not anyway . . ."

"You just sound so depressed."

"It's just Rick — that's had me in a blue funk for a while now." She slowly picked over her Mediterranean Platter with its chicken, rice, pita bread and fantastic homemade hummous.

"And they don't know . . ."

Brett raised a hand to stop Allie. "I haven't seen you in years and all you can think about is my job?"

Allie smiled back at her. "It's an easier topic than some."

Brett reached over to take her hand. "I'm sure you know loneliness better than I."

"It's strange how you never really notice and appreciate someone till they're gone."

"Isn't it?" Brett said, remembering Storm. She put her other hand on top of Allie's. Allie pulled away and paced the office. Brett stood and watched, wanting to reach out to her, but not sure how, or even if she could after all this time. "Allie." Allie stopped pacing and turned to look at Brett. Brett looked deep into her eyes, her soul. She didn't know what to do, didn't know how she could ever relieve the pain she knew Allie was going through. "You know I'm here for you, if you need me."

"Brett . . ." Allie's lips parted slightly and Brett knew she was thinking about the same thing she was — about a night five years ago.

"Are you seeing anyone?" Brett asked. It was out before she even thought about it.

Allie looked stunned at first, but then recovered. "No, I'm not."

Suddenly Allie was in Brett's arms, body against body. "I'm sorry you're alone," Brett said, hugging Allie tightly. "No one should ever be alone." She remembered how close Allie had been to her mother and her father.

There was a knock at the door.

"Come in!" Brett yelled after a momentary pause. Frankie appeared in the doorway.

"Sorry to interrupt you," Frankie began, then noticed Allie. "Allie!" he roared enthusiastically and strode across the room to give her a hearty handshake before pulling her fully into a hug.

"Frankie?" she said, surprised at his reaction.

"How ya been?"

"Okay, I guess."

"Oh," he said, looking back and forth from Brett to Allie, obviously realizing he was interrupting something. "Okay. I'm takin' off now — I'll tell you about that little 'meeting' later."

"Yeah — later this afternoon?" Brett said.

"Drinks at five — my treat."

"Gotcha."

"And I'd better see you later," Frankie said to Allie just before he turned around to leave.

Allie looked at her watch. "I'd better get going."

"Oh. Okay," Brett said, disappointed. She walked Allie down and drove her back to the House where they had left Allie's car.

"Would you . . . would you like to come over to my

place for dinner tomorrow night?" she asked, scared that Allie would decline. Instead, Allie smiled.

"Yes, yes I would, very much."

"I still live at the same place — you remember how to get there?"

"Yeah — I do."

"Good — then, how about seven?"

"That's good. It'll give me a chance to stop by home after work."

"Then it's a date?"

"It's a date."

Brett suddenly leaned forward and kissed her gently on the lips. The feeling traveled right down to Allie's knees.

ehe watched Brett retreat back to her own vehicle and thought of how the recent pictures she had seen hadn't done Brett justice. The light gray that casually graced Brett's black hair seemed to give her an air of dignity, of sobriety and respect and power. She could find nothing menacing about the image of Brett in the neatly cut suit with pleated slacks that accented the slenderness of her waist, the double-breasted jacket falling down from her broad shoulders, a white, open-collared silk shirt neatly draping her chest and highly polished loafers completing the image. The only thoughts that came to mind didn't belong there, so she quickly shoved them to the side.

She had tried practicing the shock she should see from mistakenly running into Brett. Her greatest imaginings were nothing compared with the shock that registered in every nerve of her body as soon as she saw the real, live woman, when she had looked into those hazel eyes.

Brett's kindness, especially after these few years, caught her off-guard. She had been prepared for the monster created in Randi's imagination, but instead she found Brett. Her dear, beloved Brett.

In that instant, before she even saw Storm's picture across the shelf from hers, she knew Randi was right. Brett still wanted her.

On her way home from work, Brett stopped by the store to pick up chicken breasts, olive oil, parsley, cheese, French bread, wine and a few other supplies. She stayed up late pounding the chicken for the Kiev, seasoning it with salt, pepper, onion powder and garlic. She then rolled it so that it could spend the entire night soaking up the flavors.

No one who looked at Brett Higgins would ever dream of her culinary prowess, but she had always thought a good butch should be able to do more to win a woman's heart than merely flex her muscles or change her oil. Granted, it had been quite a while since she had liked someone well enough to go to all the bother of fixing her a nice meal, but . . .

Brett tried, once again, to convince herself that she was just concerned about Allie, concerned about a friend in need, but she knew Storm was gone, and nothing she did would ever be able to change that. All she could do was try to win Allie back.

Allie was a very sensual woman — she had loved it when Brett touched her, when Brett made love to her. She would lie there, her blond eyelashes brushing her cheek, and moan out Brett's name so softly, pulling Brett tighter and tighter as she neared the edge. She made her needs known to Brett by pressing Brett's mouth closer to her own with a gentle hand to the back of Brett's head, or by pressuring Brett's hands and mouth while Brett made love to her. Brett loved the way Allie would hold her hand when she used her mouth on her, loved the connection that brought. Everything with Allie was just so easy, so natural, so comfortable. And each and every image of Allie had tormented Brett for the past five long, lonely years.

Brett wiped her eyes, which were tearing because of the onions, and pressed her forehead against the cupboards. She was almost done. Soon, she could go to sleep . . .

The ancient building had obviously seen better days. The deteriorated door gave easily after a well-placed kick from her heavy hiking boot. As it fell off its corroding hinges, the musty stench of the stagnant building wafted out to surround her and, with each step she took further propelling her into the cryptlike room, dust scattered like raven wings across the vast and dismal space. Like a vision of hell, the memories of broken promises and long-ago dreams were charred by the stinging sunlight entering from the dirt-shrouded skylight. Wall-to-wall carpet lay on the floor, its once intricate pattern worn away through years of use. Dirt encrusted the carved moldings of the walls and ceiling. At the far end of the room she saw a high arched portal, leading like the gates of hell to an unseeable visage.

She continued, even as a cloud passed over the afternoon sun, darkening the room like a cloak. The second room beckoned to her as Mary had once called to her sheep. She cautiously inched her way into the room.

Ghostly figures danced within an elaborate ballroom, disappearing here, only to reappear there and she was slowly swept up by the faint hum of a violin. As she strained into the darkness, she noticed the band off to the side, and gradually she became aware that the light did not come from another skylight, but instead from a great glass chandelier that hung precariously above.

As the room grew brighter and louder, she began to hear voices and laughter intermixed with sashaying figures on the dance floor. She studied them and found herself being turned about by their swiftly moving ballroom dancing, even as she became confused and disoriented and realized she recognized these people.

There, over there, was Cybill, dancing with Rick, and there were Allie's parents, dancing together and, and . . .

She saw herself dancing with Storm and felt a sense of impending doom.

CHAPTER 22
Out of the Frying Pan

Kirsten immediately noticed something different about Brett the next morning. There seemed to be a happy lilt to her step, a ready grin on her face and a cheerful ring to her voice. Things Kirsten hadn't seen very much in the last few years. In the last few years, a darkness had cloaked itself about Brett's shoulders. There always seemed to be something lurking deep within her dark eyes, eyes that never opened for Kirsten. Mystery had always enshrouded

Brett, but it seemed to have deepened since Storm's death and its cannibalistic qualities had increased with Rick's recent demise.

This new Brett was the Brett she had seen from a distance at PrideFest when she'd been with Allie. This Brett was happy and carefree, not at all the woman who ran one of the city's largest porn operations, among other things. Kirsten couldn't decide whether or not she liked this woman.

"You seem especially happy today," Kirsten said as Brett cut through the office. "What happened — you get laid?"

"No, you should know better than that." She was a little too quick with her reply for Kirsten's liking.

Kirsten wrapped her arms around Brett's neck and pressed her half-naked body against Brett. "So how 'bout tonight?"

"Shit — Frankie and I been working our tails off lately. When I get home, I just wanna sit down with a cold beer and watch the late movie."

"I could join you and we could watch a coupla girlie movies." Something was different, something was wrong.

"Aw shit, Kirsten." Brett pulled away. "I don't wanna take work home with me every night." When Kirsten released her, she quickly turned and launched herself up the stairs to her office. Kirsten stood watching her.

"Damn that Kirsten anyway." Brett plopped herself down in her chair.

Frankie closed the door behind them and said, "I always told you to watch your back with that one."

"Yeah, you did."

Frankie hadn't wanted Brett to give Kirsten a job, but Rick liked the idea. Brett had figured Kirsten would last one, maybe two days, tops. Then she'd get disgusted and leave.

Brett had sat in on one of Kirsten's shows the first day, as she would have with any other dancer, and watched. Kirsten met her eyes a couple of times and smiled at her, but what disturbed Brett was that Kirsten seemed to enjoy teasing the men. She seemed to enjoy flirting with them, making them hard. Brett stayed and watched Kirsten do several lap dances before she got up and went into the office to work out the next month's schedule.

After she was done dancing, and the next dancer was onstage, Kirsten came into the office wearing only a g-string. She ran her hands over Brett's shoulders and pressed her naked breasts into Brett's back. The sudden contact came as a surprise to the near celibate Brett, who moaned slightly when Kirsten straddled her lap and buried Brett's face in her breasts, until Brett abruptly stood up and went upstairs, leaving the clerk, who had witnessed the entire episode, wide-eyed.

Kirsten pursued Brett with a single-minded devotion. Soon after the remodeling was done upstairs, Brett walked into her office to discover a buck-naked Kirsten sitting on her desk with her legs spread wide, fully revealing her newly shaven pussy. She had gone there after a show and taken off her g-string while Brett was in Rick's office.

Brett had a lock put on the downstairs door, but her resistance was beginning to wear down.

"Git it while the gittin's good," was Rick's comment on the entire matter. He would've, and might've, done Kirsten at the slightest provocation.

"She's after somethin'," Frankie said. "I don' know what it is, but a woman needs a reason to act like that."

"Yeah, she's horny and needs to get laid," Rick replied.

"It's buggin' me," Brett said.

"Brett, she's makin' us a lot of money, plus she's fun to look at. Fuck her and get it over with."

Then one day Brett was watching the box office so the clerk could pick up something for lunch. As Rick was leaving, Kirsten finished her dancing and Rick let her into the office. She wasn't wearing anything except her heels and fishnet stockings. She leaned back against a wall and Rick slid his gaze up and down her. Brett snorted and turned back to her book.

"Brett," Rick said, and Brett turned back around. He spoke to her but looked at Kirsten. "When do you have our girl scheduled to dance next?" Kirsten's body was glistening with sweat. Brett pulled out the schedule book she kept in the office and looked at it. Kirsten walked up next to her and leaned over, her breasts brushing Brett's shoulder.

"Exactly one month," Brett replied not looking up. Kirsten sat on the desk and put a foot between Brett's legs on the chair. Rick grinned at this.

"Good," he said. "Kirsten, keep up the good work." She looked at him and raised an eyebrow.

"With the customers, that is." He walked out and closed the door behind him. Kirsten slid down to straddle Brett, who still sat in the chair. She put her arms on Brett's shoulders. Brett finally put her hands on Kirsten's hips, finding nowhere else to put them without looking like a fool.

"Brett, Storm's dead."

"I know that."

"And Allie ain't coming back."

"How do you know that?"

"The whole world knows it — after the break-up you two had."

"What's your point, Kirsten?"

"It's no use saving yourself for either of them." Kirsten leaned back against the desk, to better show off her breasts.

"You're not the only option."

"But I know you're not seeing anyone."

Brett considered this, and considered the naked body draped across hers. Why not?

"I'm not asking for any commitments or promises, Brett." Kirsten ran a hand through Brett's hair and down Brett's face. Brett moved her hands up Kirsten's body, feeling the swell of her tits, enjoying the silkiness of the naked skin. Kirsten breathed deeply, bringing more attention to her breasts. Brett ran her hands down over the outsides of her thighs.

"Right here and now, baby, right here and now," Kirsten said as she pulled Brett's face to her breast. Brett eagerly clamped onto the nipple, sucking it, lightly biting it, teasing it with her tongue. Kirsten moaned her appreciation. Brett pulled her roughly into her, pressing her belt buckle into Kirsten's wet pussy.

"Ooo, yes," she said as Brett picked her up and put her on the desk. Brett ran her hands roughly up and down her body as she arched in pleasure. Kirsten guided Brett's hands to her pussy where Brett ran her fingers roughly up and down the swollen, wet lips. "I want you inside me."

Brett shoved four fingers into her, trying to play rough, but Kirsten moaned and arched again, whimpering until Brett pushed her entire fist into her, pulling it in and out and twisting it around, while her other hand roughly twisted and pulled on first one then the other nipple.

"That's it baby, I like it rough, ride me hard, baby."

"My God, she's a fuckin' dyke," one of the customers said.

Brett looked over and saw several men watching them through the bullet-proof glass. Anger coursed through her, wondering if Kirsten set this up to boost her popularity. She thought about pulling out and leaving Kirsten in near-orgasmic anguish, but instead, she rammed her fist back into her, feeling Kirsten tighten around it. Kirsten squirmed on the desk, oblivious to all else except her approaching climax.

"It's like this," Brett said, pushing it in again, liking the feel and look of what she was doing to Kirsten, liking the sight of the naked body spread out just for her, liking the power she felt over Kirsten. Kirsten gasped and shuddered and gently pulled herself off of Brett's fist. She sat up quickly, trying to cover herself from the men, and looked up at Brett.

It was that look that made Brett question her hypothesis. That look told her Kirsten didn't just consider her a fun fuck. She wasn't sure what that look was, but she brought Kirsten up into her arms amidst the loud applause.

"That's all, boys," she said as she quickly carried Kirsten upstairs. That was the day Kirsten had taken Brett's college ring from her finger and put it on her own. No one but Brett had ever worn that ring, but Brett just didn't feel like fighting over it.

To this day, Brett still didn't have anything figured out about Kirsten, except that when she wanted something, she'd do anything to get it. It had taken Kirsten a while before she got Brett to spend the night with her, but when she did, Brett saw how innocent and childlike she was in her sleep. She had to keep reminding herself that Kirsten could be evil when she wanted to. She also had to keep reminding Kirsten that this was just a fling, even when it kept on going for over two years.

"Sometimes I think she wants more than your life," Frankie said.

"Huh?" Brett replied, her mind still on Kirsten and the past two years, when she had frequently shared her bed with a woman she wasn't sure she even liked very much.

"Very possessive, I don't think she's good for you. Besides, she's just a cheap slut."

"At least she made me move on from Allie and Storm." *More than her life?* Where had she heard that before?

"But don't lose Allie again over her."

"Y'know, Frankie, a coupla years ago, I wondered which was my soulmate, Allie or Storm."

"And what'd you decide?"

"I didn't. I just hope it wasn't Storm."

* * * * *

Brett got home and took a long, hot shower. She wanted to scrub away the feel of the theater. She took her time dressing, carefully selecting a silk shirt that was nice to the touch and a pair of well-washed blue jeans. She wanted to dress for Allie but didn't want Allie to know she had done so. She ran around doing a last minute tidy-up of the place and then got down to the serious issue of cooking. She put on an apron in case she splattered anything on herself. She was grateful for this added chance at Allie and didn't want to do anything to spoil it.

Allie arrived right on time and seemed nervous about coming in. They nervously hugged and Brett could feel the tension in Allie's body. "I know it's impossible to undo everything that happened, but can't we try?"

"So this is like a first date?" Allie asked, teasing a little as she relaxed.

"Second. Lunch was the first."

Brett had set the table with linen and picked up some flowers on her way home. She pulled Allie's chair out for her.

"Just becoming a little femme, huh?" Allie indicated Brett's apron.

"Shit!" Brett yanked it from her neck and tossed it into the sink. "I didn't want to mess myself up . . ." She looked into Allie's eyes.

"My God, Brett, you're making me feel special."

"You are."

* * * * *

My God, she means it, Allie thought. Brett took her hand and kissed it.

Yesterday afternoon, when Allie had returned to the station, she'd found Randi angrily pacing Greg's office.

"What was that all about?"

"What?"

"Kissing her, for God's sake."

"You were watching?"

"Yes, I was. I wanted to make sure she didn't try anything."

"Well don't. I don't want her seeing you and getting suspicious."

"I'm just trying to protect you."

"I know that, Randi." Allie hugged Randi. "It's just that I'm the one out there — and if she gets suspicious, there's no telling what she may do."

"Yeah, but . . ."

"Don't 'yeah, but' me." Allie laid a finger against Randi's lips. "I'm not sure yet, but I don't think she's been keeping tabs on me."

"So what's up?" Randi pulled away to pace the room.

"I'm meeting her for dinner tomorrow night."

"Where?"

"Her place."

"Oh, God, Allie — the woman's a killer!"

"I'm a good cop, Randi. I can watch out for myself."

"Yeah, but I'm the one who loves ya, remember? I care about what happens to you."

That was the first time Randi had ever even referred to loving Allie. Allie wasn't sure she was comfortable with the idea. "Now, don't go getting all sentimental with me. We're professionals, remember?"

Apparently Randi took the hint. She stepped away from Allie. "So she invited you to her place for dinner."

"Yes. I think she wants to give it another try."

"Her place and you don't want me to follow." Randi took her roughly by the arms. "Are you gonna sleep with her, Allie?"

Allie pulled away. "I'm not planning on it."

"But if she asks, you will." Not a question.

"Randi, if what you think is true, she's a killer. And I'm a cop. A damned good one at that — I don't need your jealousy getting in the way of my job." Allie had been planning on telling Brett she wanted to take it slow, but she didn't like this possessive side of Randi.

The next morning Greg had told Randi that all surveillance would stop, effective immediately.

"Penny for your thoughts?" Brett asked, pulling Allie back to the present.

"Just thinking about work and the strange twist that brought me here tonight." Allie glanced up and into the deep brown of Brett's eyes. She felt lost in their depth.

They finished eating and Brett said, "I can clean up later, why don't we go in the living room and talk?"

In the living room, Allie sat in a chair by the window. She noticed that nothing about the house had really changed in the past five years.

"Keeping your distance."

Allie looked at her. "Not really. I just wanted to see what it looked like outside."

"Hot and muggy." Brett put on a CD and went back to the couch.

My God, Whitney Houston, Allie thought as the music began.

"Our song," she said reflexively to Brett, who grinned. The years seemed to drop away and there sat the dashing woman who had held her in her arms all night . . .

"Will you dance with me, Miss Sullivan?" Brett extended her hand. As they began their slow dance, Allie became aware of Brett's body so close to her own. Her heart skipped a beat as she rested her chin on Brett's shoulder and placed her cheek next to Brett's. Brett pulled back a little and looked into Allie's eyes. "Forever and ever."

"What?"

"You're wearing Eternity — as in, forever and ever."

Allie wondered if this is what it felt like when two souls met. Brett ran her hand down Allie's back, then rested it on Allie's hip, apparently not daring to go further. Her other hand stroked Allie's hair and played in its curls.

At the end of the song, they stopped dancing and stood touching each other and looking into each other's eyes. Allie began to pull away and Brett stepped back and bowed.

"Thank you for the dance, m'lady," she said, still holding onto Allie's hand. She finally released it and went to sit on the couch. Allie sat next to her. They talked until 2 a.m., when Allie finally couldn't stifle any more yawns.

"Oh, I'm sorry," Brett said, reaching out to touch her shoulder.

Allie looked at her watch, amazed at the time. "It's okay — it's just way past my bedtime. I should get going." Neither of them moved. Brett slowly brushed her hand over Allie's cheek and traced her lips with her finger. Allie kissed her fingers. She looked up at Brett. Those hazel eyes.

"I don't want this night to end," Brett said.

"There's always tomorrow."

Brett walked Allie out to her car and she stood watching as Allie started the engine and rolled down the window. She leaned on the windowsill, reached in and pulled Allie's head forward. She gingerly brushed her lips over Allie's. Allie responded, parting her lips slightly, allowing Brett's tongue into her mouth. She enjoyed the warmth, the closeness, the intimacy of the moment.

Brett pulled away. "Drive safely — you have valuable cargo."

Allie drove up Ryan and a tear slid down her cheek, although she didn't know why. She was glad Brett hadn't made any further overtures, because she wasn't sure she could say no.

Allie stumbled into work at ten the next morning. Randi had called to wake her at nine. She walked into Greg's office to find him sitting behind his desk with Randi pacing in front of it.

"Late night, huh?" Randi said, angrily. Greg shot her a look.

"What's up, Sullivan?" he asked.

"Nothing much," she replied with careful nonchalance as she seated herself in front of his desk. "I went over to Brett's last night for dinner and then we sat around and talked for several hours."

"What time did you leave there?" Randi asked.

"About two or three."

"And all you did was talk?"

"Randi," Greg said, "will you calm down — we want Brett to take her back. This is a good thing."

"Did you find out anything?" Randi sat down across from Allie.

"For God's sake, Randi — I don't expect her to jump right up and confess!" The good mood Allie felt was quickly leaving her.

"So what'd you two talk about?" Greg asked, his tone and eyes saying he was curious about Randi's apparent belligerence.

"Politics, current affairs, a little bit of business, not much. She kept changing the subject when I asked her about work."

The phone rang, saving Allie from the situation. Greg answered it and spoke only briefly before hanging up. He jotted a few notes on his blotter before looking up at Randi.

"That was your cousin, seems Sullivan just got a dozen red roses sent to her at the store."

"Was there a card attached?" Randi leaned forward.

"Yes. 'Thanks for last night, Brett.' "

"Thanks for last night?" Randi turned to Allie.

"We talked, that was it." Allie's heart was racing. Brett sent her roses.

"Nobody says 'thanks for last night' about a conversation, Allie."

"Okay, we kissed as I was leaving." Damn Randi and her curiousity. She'd never be able to understand how she felt when she looked into Brett's eyes, when Brett touched her.

"Are you sure that's all you did for her?"

"Randi," Greg interrupted. "If that's what Allie says happened, that's what happened. Have I ever given you the third degree over a surveillance?"

"This is different! I don't think Allie realizes how dangerous Brett is . . ."

A plainclothes officer entered the room and handed Greg a folder. Greg took it, nodded, and the officer left. He leaned back and glanced through the folder. Allie and Randi watched with interest.

"It seems that our friend Frankie's still making the rounds," Greg said a few minutes later. "One of our contacts saw one of the exchanges last night."

"He's been trying to find out who did Rick," Randi explained to Allie.

"And two more men are in the hospital." Greg looked up at Randi and Allie. "Frankie doesn't fool around when he's serious."

"Why don't these people press charges then?" Allie asked.

"Because they're too damned afraid!" Randi suddenly roared.

Allie didn't like the look in Randi's eyes. "I'm getting some coffee."

"Sullivan, I want a daily report on what's happening," Greg said as she left. She waved her acknowledgment.

The next morning Brett was in a cheerful mood, which was unusual for her in the mornings. Kirsten seemed to notice this.

"You're in kinda late, especially after leaving early yesterday," Kirsten said, immediately pouncing on her like some sort of deranged jungle animal.

"Not all of my work is centered on this building," was all Brett would tell her.

"What are you doin' tonight?" Kirsten asked.

"Frankie and I got some business to take care of."

"You're never gonna find Rick's killer."

"How would you know?"

"Brett, in a town this size, with the number of people who would have had a reason to want Rick dead . . ."

"We will find him."

"How do you know it's a him?" There was something in her eyes that scared Brett. Something she not only didn't like, but didn't trust.

"Do you know something we don't?"

"No, just speculation."

Brett left her in the office and bounded upstairs, making sure to lock the door behind her. She found Frankie in his office. "Frankie, you gotta cover for me."

"What's up?" He glanced up from his doodling.

"I told Kirsten I was gonna be with you tonight."

She paused, waiting for him to say anything. "Really, I'm taking Allie out for dinner and dancing."

He grinned at her. "Yeah, I'll cover for you."

She smiled and nodded. "What's up with Rick?"

"Nothin'. Fuckin' nothin'. Somebody's hidin' somethin', and I'm gonna find out what."

"What're you gonna do?"

"I'm thinkin' maybe I should start askin' around here. Maybe somebody heard or saw somethin' that'll tell me where I should ask next." He leaned back and cracked his knuckles. Brett turned to leave. "Hey, Brett." Frankie leaned back and looked at his watch. "You get lucky last night?"

"Yes, but not the way you think."

"You fucked her, didn't you?" Randi said, catching Allie outside in the parking lot.

"Leave me alone, Randi."

Randi stood and watched Allie drive off. *Not again. No, not again, Brett.*

CHAPTER 23
Foiled Again

Brett picked Allie up at her house and they went to the Whitney for an elegant dinner before going dancing at the Railroad Crossing. When they arrived at the bar it was still rather early so the crowd was light. They danced a few fast songs, bopping to the beat of the top 40 dance mix. They finally sat down and were enjoying a drink in a quiet corner of the bar, but Brett kept glancing over Allie's shoulder, and

Allie noticed it, but didn't really pay any attention to it.

"It's been a while since I've been here." Brett leaned back with her drink, a slight smile playing across her lips.

"I was coming here kinda regular for a bit, but then I just wasn't really in the mood."

"I don't blame you." Brett took Allie's hand and kissed it.

"Allie!" a woman yelled, running up from behind to give her a hug.

"Lara, how're you doin'?"

"I'm fine, and yourself?" Lara asked, noticing Brett.

"Okay. Lara, this is Brett, Brett, this is Lara."

"Pleased to meet you." Brett stood and warmly shook hands with Lara. Something once again grabbed her attention. "Will you ladies excuse me just one moment?" she asked, striding off. Allie turned to watch, and was stunned by what she saw: Randi was at a table facing them.

"Isn't that the woman who was hitting on you the last time we met here?" Lara asked.

"Yes, it is," Allie replied, watching Brett lean on a chair and get in Randi's face. Damn her, anyway. She wasn't supposed to be watching. Randi appeared uninterested with what Brett was saying. Brett pointed and Allie could almost hear her voice. Finally, Brett grabbed Randi's ear and twisted it so Randi's head was down on the table. Allie gasped as she saw Randi reaching for something she, Allie, knew was her gun. She was gonna blow it.

Suddenly, a bouncer walked up and pulled Brett

away from Randi, who stood up, rubbing her ear. Brett said something to the bouncer and the bouncer looked at the two women, stopping Randi as she tried to grab Brett. Finally, Randi stormed off and out the door. Brett handed a few bills to the bouncer and came back shaking her head.

"What was that about?" Allie asked as she returned.

"That woman's been starin' at you all night — when we were dancing, when we were talking . . . So I figured I'd let her know that annoyed me."

"She was hitting on Allie a coupla weeks ago," Lara offered.

"Was she?"

"Yeah, and I told her I wasn't interested."

"She looks real familiar . . ."

"Don't you know, Brett," Lara offered with a smile, "we all look alike."

"Let's dance." Allie stood and took Brett's hand.

The next morning, Allie confronted Randi.

"You agreed you wouldn't watch her."

"I wasn't. I do occasionally go to the bars, you know."

"Then why were you staring at us?"

"I wasn't thinking. I was just surprised to see you two there."

"You want me in public places, then you almost blow my cover when I go to one!"

"If you told me where you were going we wouldn't have this problem." Randi sipped her coffee. They were standing in the kitchen of Randi's apartment. Allie looked around at the dirty dishes, the smelly litter box and the laundry strewn throughout the apartment. Half-empty glasses, beer and soda cans and magazines were spread throughout it all.

"I've been too busy to clean."

"You almost pulled your gun on her."

"I was worried. I didn't know what she'd do."

"She wouldn't do anything in a public place. Besides, I'm not doin' all this work for my own good. I don't want you to blow our cover so all we end up with is an assault and battery."

"You're right, hon." Randi pulled Allie into her arms. "Next time I see you two, I'll just leave."

Allie sighed and rested her head on Randi's shoulder. She was tired. The day's humidity was already bearing down on her like a tyrannosaurus, and she didn't know who or what to believe, but she didn't really trust Randi and had a feeling Randi wasn't telling her something. What had she ever seen in her in the first place? All she knew was that now was not the time to break up with her. There was no telling what she'd do if she did.

Kirsten pushed her damp hair back from her brow. She was thankful it was Sunday. Her week was over and she could find out what was up with Brett.

She was crouched in a bush across the street from Brett's house. She had been there for three hours already and still there was no sign of Brett. It was a hot and humid day and she was sweating like one of those repairmen who walk around showing off their fuzzy butt cracks.

Things hadn't been right with Brett all week and Kirsten knew something was up, although she wasn't quite sure what it was. She had a feeling there was another woman involved. That was the reason for the stakeout. Kirsten hadn't come this far to be replaced by some cheap floozy. Years ago she had known it would take quite a woman to lay claim to Brett, to get Brett to settle for just one woman. Storm hadn't been able to do it, and neither had Allie, but she knew she could. And Brett should know better than to ever even look at another woman while she belonged to Kirsten.

She had parked two streets over and trekked through a couple of yards to make sure Brett had no chance of knowing she was watching. If only she'd show up, she thought. Her legs were cramping something awful and the briars were beginning to prick her. She just couldn't get comfortable. She just wanted to go home and relax in her air conditioning, maybe even hit the pool.

She looked up and saw Brett's black Aurora pull into the driveway. Someone was in the passenger's seat, but she couldn't tell who it was. Kirsten's jaw dropped as a woman climbed out of the car and walked hand in hand with Brett up the walkway, with Brett holding a large shopping bag in her free hand. Although Kirsten couldn't see the face, she could see the hair, the figure and the attitude. At the front door, the woman obligingly turned to look across the street as Brett pulled out her keys.

Allie.

* * * * *

Brett ushered Allie into the house. They had decided to fool the day and spend it at a movie and shopping at Oakland Mall. Now Brett adjusted the air conditioning, turning it up a bit higher to stave off the humidity.

Allie flopped down on the couch and smiled at Brett. Brett hadn't realized how unhappy she'd been until this past week. She'd been happy this week, and everyone had noticed it, including the dancers, even Cherie, the one who was usually half-drugged out.

She'd almost forgotten how it felt to be happy.

She looked at Allie and smiled back. She thought about something she hadn't really considered for years, not really since prom night. She thought about retiring — letting Frankie buy her out, slowly teaching him and phasing herself out. He'd do all right on his own. She could go back to school and get her M.B.A. Maybe move to California, start all over again with Allie. She knew she loved her, had never stopped loving her. They could both use a fresh start.

She looked at Allie, noticed the tanned legs beneath the shorts, the slight sweat on her upper chest above her shirt, the swell of her shirt a little further down. Brett wanted to take it slowly; she didn't want to overwhelm her.

Allie had asked her several questions about business over the past week, but she didn't really want to pull Allie into all that. At first she didn't know why, but then she realized she wasn't proud of all she had built. She wasn't proud of many of the things she had done over the past years, things that sometimes kept her up at night, things that drove her to drown her life in a bottle of scotch, things that the idealistic girl of a decade ago wouldn't even dream of doing. She had become a pessimist, always looking at the down side, always devaluing everything.

"Whatcha thinking, babe?" Allie asked.

"About life, work and us." She sat next to Allie. "What do you think about California?"

"It's nice. At least their weather is usually more predictable — but I'd miss the seasons."

Brett looked at her. "There's something I want you to have." She reached into her pocket and pulled out the key ring she had given Allie the one Christmas they were together. Allie took it and ran her fingers over it.

"You kept it."

The last time Allie had seen it, she was throwing it across a room at Brett. "I don't want to lose you again, Allie." Brett leaned down to kiss Allie's soft lips. She let her lips travel along the line of Allie's jaw, then down her neck, kissing away the day's sweat. She looked up at Allie.

"Cat's eyes," Allie whispered, noticing as if for the first time the color of Brett's eyes.

Brett licked her lips. "I want to make love to you," she said, watching Allie. Allie slowly nodded, and Brett picked her up in her arms and carried her into the bedroom.

They slowly undressed each other in the half light provided by the nearly closed blinds. Brett pulled off Allie's shirt and undid her bra, slowly cupping her breasts. She nuzzled and kissed them, pulling the nipples into her mouth, enjoying the taste and feel.

She had forgotten how soft and pert those breasts were.

Allie pulled out Brett's shirt and ran her hands up her back. Brett undid Allie's shorts and pulled them down before lifting her onto the bed. She sat back and looked at Allie's naked body, slowly running her hands over the satiny skin, enjoying the curves and swells. She reached around and took off her own shirt and bra, so she could lie on top of Allie and place her naked breasts on Allie's body.

Allie gasped as Brett lay on top of her. Brett could feel her every breath. She began kissing Allie's shoulders, slowly working her tongue and lips over the naked body, hearing Allie's every moan, every breath. She paused to play with her nipples, sucking them and flitting her tongue back and forth over them. She lightly nibbled the area just above Allie's belly button, then ran her chin over Allie's furry mound.

Allie arched as Brett opened her outer lips to look at the tender moist hidden folds. Brett gently blew on the tender tip before running her tongue up and down Allie's swollen clit. Brett put her tongue inside, enjoying the tangy taste of her, enjoying the feel of her movements against her hands and body. She began to slowly run her tongue up and down as she placed two fingers inside of Allie. Her fingers were warm and Allie moaned again as she spread her legs wider still, holding onto Brett's free hand.

Brett thought Allie was reacting like a woman who hadn't been made love to in a while, like a woman who hadn't been truly enjoyed in several years.

As Brett flicked her tongue with more force across Allie's clit, she pulled her slightly bent fingers in and out, feeling Allie's increased arousal. She felt Allie's legs begin to tighten around her neck, as her insides began to tighten around her fingers. She increased the force in her tongue, and the rapidity of her fingers in and out.

"Oh God." Allie moaned. "Oh God, oh God."

Brett's tongue moved faster still, concentrating on the hidden nugget at the top of Allie's clit. She sucked it into her mouth as she beat it with her tongue, as she felt Allie's g-spot with her fingers.

"Brett!"

Brett slowly pulled her fingers out and ran her tongue up and down Allie's clit, enjoying the tastes, the feeling. She slowly raised herself up and moved next to Allie on the bed. She pulled Allie into her arms. A tear ran down Allie's cheek and she gently wiped it away. "I love you."

CHAPTER 24
Making the Moves

"It's been over two weeks now, Greg," Randi said when she had him alone.

"These things take time, Randi."

"She's not telling us everything."

"How would you know?"

"I just know, okay?"

Greg leaned back in his chair and chewed on his pencil, as if he should've known better than to try to give up smoking now. "Randi, you know I don't usually ask you about your personal life . . ."

"And it's appreciated."

"But I need to know — is there something going on with you and Allie?"

"I preferred it when you didn't ask questions," Randi said, hoping he couldn't tell how she felt about Allie. She knew he must think she was jealous, but how else was she supposed to act? After all, she loved Allie, although she had only ever referred to it, not actually said it. How could she have ever fallen so hard for a woman who so obviously enjoyed everything that was the antithesis of her?

"You've been too concerned with precise details of little shit like kissing. These two were a couple. For all we know, they had a fucking wonderful sex life, and that's all."

"Brett wants her back." Who wouldn't? She was so responsive in bed, so passionate. Of course, that was probably all Brett ever saw in her.

"But maybe it's just for the sex."

"I don't want her to get hurt."

"It's more than that."

"I think Allie should make her move."

"How do you suppose she should do that?"

"She's got a key to Brett's house. She could search it." Randi said what she had been thinking about since that night at the bar. "She's known around the theater. They wouldn't ask questions if she showed up early and searched the offices. She could wear a bug . . ."

"And wait for Brett to confess, I suppose?"

"We've got to do something, Greg. I can't stand

sitting around and waiting. At least let me follow Brett, or Allie."

"You promised Allie —"

"For God's sake, Greg, she could end up in trouble. It's just this feeling I've got, and what she don't know won't hurt her." She wanted this over and done with. She wasn't sure which she wanted more — Allie's love or Brett's death.

"I'll think about it."

"You've got to do something, Allie," Randi said over lunch.

Allie looked at her coolly. Randi was beginning to get on Allie's nerves. Whenever Allie wasn't with Brett, Randi wanted to be with her. She was being pos- sessive, and Allie didn't like playing both sides of the fence.

"I don't think she did it."

"Regardless, we know she's done enough to get her a decade or so."

"But I thought you wanted the whole ball of wax."

"I do. But Greg's getting pressure and we're thinking about bringing her in for questioning on DeSilva."

Allie toyed with her silverware. "This isn't as easy as you seem to think it is. It takes time to get someone's trust. To get them to tell you things."

"That's why we picked you, because she already knows you. Every night we wait, Frankie's beating up more people. Every second it takes, somebody gets hurt. And there's no telling what they're planning next. Brett's an ambitious woman. I don't think she's planning on stopping with just DeSilva's operation."

"I need more time, Randi." Allie met Randi's eyes with what she hoped was sincerity. She had to keep Greg and Randi from pulling Brett in. She didn't want them to be able to implicate her in anything, and she didn't want Brett to know what her original intentions were. She had to convince Randi she was holding nothing back. She was sure she could reform Brett.

This left her wondering why she had become a cop in the first place.

"Frankie!" Brett called from her office.

"Yeah?" he said, sticking his head in.

"Get in here."

"Whatsa matter?"

"Nothin', I just figured I should start letting you know more about what I do."

"Why? You need some help?"

"Yeah, that and, well, I'm thinkin' of retiring."

"Retiring? Why?"

"I'm beginning to think maybe this isn't the life for me. I want something nice and peaceful where I don't have to watch my back and don't have to worry about what I say all the time."

"It's Allie, isn't it?" Frankie had a slight smile on his lips.

"Yeah. I don't want to pull her into all this."

"I don't blame you. She's a nice girl. And you've loved her too long to let it go for this joint."

"You notice more than you're supposed to." Brett wasn't surprised.

"It's part of my job. Have you said anything to her?"

"I haven't told anyone. I want to start setting things up, though."

"Where'll you go to?"

"I think California — I want a nice house with a white picket fence."

"I'll miss you."

"Aw, don't go saying shit like that. Y'know we have to keep up appearances." Brett studied the big lug's face, knowing he was the one true friend she had, knowing the heart it took for someone who so obviously loved her to let her go.

The phone rang.

"You get it, Frankie."

"Yeah?" he said, answering it. "She's on the other line, Kirsten." He paused, listening. "No, we already ate — we're digging through Rick's stuff. Brett's lookin' for something important." He listened again, said, "Yeah," and hung up. He looked at Brett. "She wanted to go to lunch with you."

"Figured as much." Brett looked around. "I should start organizing everything up here, though."

"You gotta do somethin' about her, Brett."

"I know, Frankie. God knows, I know," she replied, thinking that trouble was brewing, but she wasn't sure just what.

Randi watched Kirsten enter the theater. She knew she was taking a chance, but she needed something to happen, soon. She pulled her car into the lot and parked next to Kirsten's light blue Camry, taking her time before getting out. She wanted to give Kirsten a headstart. She popped the hood, checked her oil, kicked her tires and checked her lights before she headed to the theater.

Just inside the door, before the turnstile, she looked into the office and saw Kirsten hang up the phone, disgusted. She slowly pulled out her wallet as the clerk came up to the window and Kirsten banged out the door. Kirsten looked at her.

"Venus!" Randi called Kirsten by her stage name.

"Do I know you?" Kirsten looked Randi up and down.

"I'm from out of town, and one of my friends has been writing to me about you."

"She has?"

"He, actually. We grew up together. He sent me a picture of you."

"Well, I'm not working today."

"You're not?" Randi tried to seem disappointed. "I really wanted to see you perform, after all he's said."

Kirsten looked at her. Randi could tell that Kirsten was sizing her up, perhaps even comparing her with Brett. "What are you doing for lunch?"

"Nothing. Can I take you somewhere?"

Over lunch, as Randi sang her praises, Kirsten revealed her real name. She had had to do some quick thinking, though. Kirsten had noticed her plates, so she explained that she had grown up in the area and moved to Traverse City later on. She tried to show that she was very interested in Kirsten. Perhaps they could schedule a private performance, since she had driven all that way to see her?

Kirsten's exact connection to Brett had somehow eluded Greg and Randi for quite a while. They hadn't mentioned her to Allie but had done some additional digging on her instead. What they came up with, that Kirsten and Brett were most likely lovers, intrigued Randi enough to set up this morning's activities. If she couldn't follow Brett or Allie, at least she could try to tie up any loose ends. Who knew what she knew? She'd probably been sleeping with Brett for a couple of years.

"I think that could be arranged," Kirsten said finally.

"I'm staying with my friend, so maybe we should get a motel."

A few hours later, they lay in bed, sweaty from their exertions, and Kirsten sat up to get a cigarette. She handed one to Randi and rejoined her in bed. It was a cheap motel, located just off I-696 in Warren, an okay neighborhood but nothing fancy. Randi didn't want to take a chance on anyone catching them together, so she talked Kirsten into going to a motel in a suburb.

"What's it like — doing what you do?" Randi rolled over to face Kirsten.

"Interesting. I get to meet all sorts of people."

"What sorts?"

"They're mostly perverts, but I got 'em wrapped around my finger. They'd do just about anything for me," Kirsten said with a grin. She paused. "And they have."

"Do you often give such special service?" Randi indicated the tossed sheets and clothes.

"No. I don't really like guys. I won't do 'em for just money."

"So I was a special case?" Randi wondered what Kirsten meant by that.

"Yeah," Kirsten answered, considering her, "you're cute, plus my old lady ain't been givin' me any lately."

"Your old lady?"

"She owns the theater."

"A woman owns it?"

"Yeah, everybody knows her — Brett Higgins."

"Isn't this dangerous then? Seeing as that's where we met?"

"Not really. An old girlfriend just showed up and she's been acting like an idiot about her."

"What about you?"

"That's what I want to know. Goddamned bitch doesn't give a shit about everything I've done for her. I should've dealt with Allie while I had a chance. I shoulda just handled her right from the start."

"Whaddya mean?" Randi asked, trying not to appear too curious. She had always heard people were liable to say anything after sex, and that probably went double for the really great sex they had just had, but she never thought it was true . . .

"Allie would never do what I've done for Brett. Allie is a selfish little bitch who only puts herself first."

"Allie is the ex?"

"Yeah, Allie is the ex. I broke them up once before, but she just won't take a hint. She could never do for Brett what I've done."

Randi watched as Kirsten got up, not bothered by her nakedness, and opened the curtain to look out. It was the second time she'd brought up "all I've done for Brett." And what did she mean about breaking them up? Randi wondered.

"Gonna rain soon," Kirsten said, looking out the window. "At least it'll cut the humidity, maybe cool things down a bit. I just hope it starts soon."

"It sounds to me like Brett just doesn't appreciate what she's got."

Kirsten looked at her. "No, she doesn't." She paused. "You still have a lot of friends around here?"

"No, just Paul. I live up north now and I really like it. I only come down once a year to visit him for a couple of days."

Kirsten lit another cigarette. "I dated Allie years ago, before Brett ever showed up. I was really jealous when she did. I wanted Allie back, God knows why. I couldn't figure it out when she hooked up with Brett. Then I saw Brett's ambition, her knowledge, her power. That's when I knew Brett and I belonged together. There's no telling what the two of us can do, together."

Was she implying what Randi thought she was implying?

Kirsten lay naked on the bed next to Randi, smoking her cigarette. "Through the years, I've gotten even with Allie in my own way. But she has no idea of my power, or what I can do to her. She will now."

CHAPTER 25
Women Scorned

Randi again looked at the photo. It really wasn't a bad picture. Brett would've liked it. She was wearing a double-breasted black man's suit, tailored to fit while hiding any bulges that needed hiding. She wore a white silk shirt with a slender, patterned tie. Obviously on the way to a meeting, Brett carried an expensive leather briefcase and wore mirrored sunglasses. Randi had pulled this particular picture from a roll before she gave it to Greg a week ago. She had briefly thought about using it as a dartboard, but decided that might be a little too crazed, regard- less of her feelings about Brett Higgins.

"Damn her," she mumbled under her breath, staring at the photo. She had to decide what to do. When she left Kirsten that afternoon, she assured her that everything she had said would remain in strictest confidence. She then walked through the zoo, thinking.

Kirsten had all but confessed to several of the murders Randi had blamed on Brett: first Storm and Cybill, then Rick DeSilva.

This left Randi in a quandary. Should she tell Greg? Should she tell Allie?

Brett was still a criminal, any way she looked at it. She wanted Brett to get what she deserved and stop her from hurting anyone else. But all the attention would switch to catching Kirsten if she told anyone what she knew. The one thing Randi knew for certain was that she wanted Brett, even if for crimes she didn't commit, because there were enough crimes Randi knew Brett *had* committed — like killing her brother, Dany, those five years ago . . .

Tears stained her face and she angrily wiped her eyes with her sleeve.

The doorbell rang. Randi knew it was Allie. She had left word for Allie to get over to her place, knowing Allie wouldn't find it suspicious. Greg was attending a convention in Chicago for a long weekend. He had no idea what was up and Randi couldn't find a reason to let him know. This one had always been her baby and she was going to finish it while that wishy-washy wimp was out of the way. She closed the door to the room and went to let Allie in.

Allie barely stepped in before looking at Randi. "What do you need?"

"You have a date with Brett tonight, right?"

"Yeah . . ."

"Where are you meeting her?"

"At the theater."

"Greg wants you to wear a bug tonight. And show up early — so you can look through her office."

"Why didn't he tell me this himself?"

"He's in Chicago, at a meeting. I just got off the phone with him. We've got to make our move, or else it could go on like this for ages, Allie."

"Y'know she's not gonna confess . . ."

"Try your best. If we can even determine clear-cut motives, we'll be a lot further than we are. We want this wrapped up, soon, Allie. If Brett's not responsible, we want to know who is."

"What am I supposed to look for, in her office?"

"Double sets of books — indications of money laundering, drug dealing, child porn . . ."

"I know Brett's not involved in that."

"She's a changed woman, Allie, a changed woman." Damn, she had to convince Allie of this. She didn't want Allie hurt, but she wanted Brett — and she had tonight all lined up, had done all the planning and preparation that afternoon. She knew this was her chance, because Greg was out of town and unreachable. She wanted Brett dead before anyone else could think to get Kirsten talking. Allie was the only one of her people left to prepare.

"Greg knows about all this?"

"Yes. He helped me put it together."

"Why didn't he tell me himself?"

"He's real busy right now — if this works out, he may get a job offer from Chicago."

"Leave Detroit?"

"Yeah, but Chicago sure needs work."

Randi went with Allie to the station to pick up the bug and other equipment, then followed her to her house to help her get ready. She had to tape the wires in place and make sure her clothing was appropriate to both the occasion and the equipment.

Allie walked her out to her car. "I'll leave here in a couple of minutes. I just need to sit and have a drink by myself."

"Don't take long and don't drink much." Randi looked up at the sky. "This one's gonna be nasty." Storm clouds gathered in all their fury, rolling into each other in all their darkness.

"'It was a dark and stormy night . . .'" Allie was apparently trying to hide what she was feeling.

"Be careful tonight." Randi reached out to Allie. "Just say 'Pandora's Box' if you need us there right away."

"Pandora's Box — got it."

"Don't get yourself hurt." Randi gave Allie a quick peck on the cheek before climbing into her car and driving off.

CHAPTER 26
When the Dancing Stops

The elements were beginning to give the night a Fourth of July feeling and the rain was just starting as Brett walked into the bar.

"What do you need to talk to me about?" Brett said, wiping off a chair across from Frankie at the corner table. The grungy place was not the type Brett usually frequented.

"Sorry about the joint." Frankie pushed a Labatt's Blue Ice across the table for Brett.

"It's okay, I just have a date with Allie tonight and don't want to mess up my clothes."

"God." Frankie shook his head. "Is this the same Brett I moved more'n one body around with?"

"The things a woman does to you. Why'd you want to meet me here?"

"I wanted to make sure we weren't disturbed — or overheard."

This got her attention. "What's up?"

"It's about Storm, Cybill and one Rick De-Silva . . ."

Allie was caught in the downpour as she scurried into the theater. She held her bag over her head to keep her hair dry. If she had to do this, she at least wanted to look good while she did it.

"Hey, Sal," she said to the clerk who greeted her. He got up and let her into the theater office.

"She said she may be a bit late, didn't say why," Sal said, sitting back down. "She left the door unlocked. And left this for you." He handed Allie a note. Allie ripped open the sealed envelope and pulled out the note:

I think Frankie's onto something. I'll be here as soon as I can.
Go up and have yourself a drink.
You are my everything.

Brett

Allie hurried up the stairs, knowing she didn't have much time. A cold chill ran down Allie's spine as she remembered the mysterious phone call on the day of her father's funeral. Remembered Brett would've known about her father's nickname for her. She thought about that and what Randi had said about Brett's changing. She didn't know what to believe, although her heart told her what was right.

Allie was relieved that Randi was finally mentioning the possibility of other suspects. She had been beginning to wonder if Randi was merely obsessed with Brett.

She had been wracking her brains, trying to remember any hiding places in the offices. Brett's office was the only one unlocked. She quickly went through the files, glancing at any books and ledgers she came across. She didn't know much about bookkeeping but, as far as she could tell, everything she came across was on the up and up.

She pulled a set of lock picks out of her bag and approached Frankie's office door. She was a bit rusty with them but had the door open in just a few minutes. She turned on the light and looked around at the messy barrenness. She looked down the hallway at Rick's old office, quickly deciding that anything she found in Frankie's office would most likely point to Frankie's illicit activities and while that may be worthwhile, it was not her priority tonight. She walked down the hall to Rick's office, hoping it hadn't been cleared out yet.

She tried Rick's door and, not suprised in the least, found it locked. Gaining momentum with the picks, she had the door open in pretty good time. She turned on the light and let her gaze wander over the surroundings.

It was nicer than she remembered but, of course, it had probably been redecorated when Brett's and Frankie's offices were done. Across the front, by the window, was a large desk with papers neatly piled on it. Against the back wall were two large filing cabinets with a bookshelf covering most of the wall across from her. The wall beside her had a large Oriental carpet on it, with a sofa, two end tables and a bar against it. Two expensive-looking metal chairs sat facing the desk.

She thought about starting with the filing cabinets but then glanced back at the Oriental rug on the wall. She walked over and began to push it to the side. It was heavier than she'd expected; she'd have to pull it down.

A few moments later she was facing a neat wall safe. Kinda obvious, but who'da thunk it? Rick had never been known for extreme creativity. She examined the dial and looked at her watch. No way could she crack it. She'd have to figure out another way.

"You're the one who stands to gain the most — think about it, Brett," Frankie said, looking across the table at her.

"You think I did it? Frankie! I loved Storm almost as much as I loved Rick!" She couldn't believe she was admitting it, but it was the truth. And she also knew she loved Allie and would do whatever she had to to make sure she didn't come to the same end as almost everyone else she had ever cared about.

"Calm down, I don't think you did it. But I can't find any tracks or traces — which means it probably wasn't a professional job."

"An amateur's trying to set me up?"

"Not set you up." Frankie looked into Brett's eyes and took a sip of his drink. "I think an amateur's out to do a whole lot more than that."

Kirsten parked in a nearby lot. She was in a bad mood. Randi had looked so much like Brett, and Kirsten had enjoyed closing her eyes and imagining it was Brett wanting her so much, so badly. She needed Brett now. Needed Brett to need her, to want her like that.

But she didn't see Brett's car in the lot, only Allie's.

Allie had ripped through Rick's office, searching for the combination. She knew she was missing the obvious but couldn't think of it.

She got down on the floor and crawled underneath the desk. On the bottom of the desk she found the digits of Brett's birthday written out. Hoping she had it, knowing she did, she walked over to the safe and carefully turned the knob, listening to the tumblers within. The door slid open with only a slight thunk.

That was when she heard it. A creak in the floorboards near the office. Holding the door of the opened safe slightly ajar, she turned to face the person she was sure was Brett.

Brett swerved through the traffic, maneuvering swiftly on the roads, even though it was fast approaching flooding conditions. She swore as she almost lost control near a backed up sewer. She knew she should take care, but she couldn't stop.

What Frankie told her just made too much sense. She knew Kirsten had been totally obsessed with Allie a few years back. After all, Kirsten had screwed with Allie's life before, with some sort of affair or another. Granted, an affair was a far cry from murder, but somehow she could see it. And she also knew Kirsten now wanted her with even more fervor, and that Kirsten seemed like someone obsessed with power and money.

Frankie had expounded on the details even as Brett reasoned her own way through it all. She knew Kirsten had been at the theater earlier, but she hadn't heard from her since. And now, Allie was supposed to be at the theater waiting for her . . .

Did Kirsten know Allie was in the picture? And if so, how far would she go to get her out and keep her out?

Brett swore as she swerved into the left turn lane to avoid the sudden traffic jam. There had to be a better way than this . . .

The thunder crashed and lightning streaked the sky. Mother Nature wasn't happy about something.

* * * * *

"What have we here?" Kirsten looked at Allie, who stood next to the open safe. Allie noticed Kirsten had a gun in her hand. It was pointed at her.

"What do you want, Kirsten?"

"I want to know what you're doing tearing Rick's office apart?" Her eyes wandered only long enough to take in the entire scene. "Did our little kitten grow up to be a cop after all?"

That tone of voice, those words — the only other person who called Allie "kitten" was her dad, her dad and . . . The unknown phone caller.

"I'm waiting."

"You made the call," Allie said with dead certainty.

"I told you you'd end up alone. I just couldn't resist rubbing it in when I read the obituaries."

"You're insane." Allie stared slack-jawed across the room at Kirsten.

"No more than anybody else," Kirsten replied with a slight grin. "I'm only looking out for number one."

Allie leapt forward in a sudden movement. Unfortunately, Kirsten anticipated this and sidestepped, so Allie flew into the wall. She then jumped forward and held the gun to Allie's head.

"'Oh, Brett, I'm so so sorry,'" she mimicked what she would later say. "'I heard a noise in Rick's office, which I know is always locked, and then I shot! Such a pity.'"

"You're going to kill me?"

"I didn't kill Rick just for kicks, you know," Kirsten almost bragged. "I got Brett her little promotion, and another one's on the way — wait'll you see what I've got planned for Jack O'Rourke. Brett is going places, but not with you."

It took Randi and Scott, her partner for tonight, a bit to make out Kirsten's voice over the din of music from the show going on just below the office in the theater. They couldn't hear what was being said, though. It wasn't until Brett literally slid up to the front door in her black Aurora that they called for backup.

Brett raced from her car and Randi was sure she was pulling a gun.

"Shit!" Randi jumped from the car and dodged across the street.

Kirsten allowed Allie to stand up.

"A fitting night to die, don't you think?" she asked, pointing out the window. "I didn't do all that for Brett to lose her, you know."

"Why Storm and Cybill?"

"Cybill was in the way, and I needed Storm outta the picture."

Allie heard a creak in the hallway. Kirsten lifted the gun, pointing it right between Allie's eyes. Allie had never hoped so much to see Randi.

"Enough said, I need to get on with business, and Brett should be back at any time . . ."

Brett hurled herself through the doorway and brought her gun down on Kirsten's head. Kirsten crumpled to the floor like a dead fish. Allie ran to her, gratefully.

"Oh God, Allie." Brett wrapped her arms around her.

That was when the bells started. Bells that were set up to warn everybody when the police raided the place. Brett stopped to listen to the alarm the clerk downstairs must've set off. She looked out the window. Allie turned to see what Brett was watching and noticed, between flashes of lightning, the flashing red lights outside the theater.

"The cops?" She looked in amazement at Allie, then tossed her to the floor. "You did join 'em!" she yelled, her face unreadable, before running to the window. Before Allie knew what was happening, Brett had disappeared out it.

Allie heard a door breaking downstairs as she ran to the window, grabbing her gun. It wasn't supposed to happen like this — Kirsten had confessed to the murders! And now Brett knew she had betrayed her. She looked up to see that Brett had shimmied up a rather strong drainpipe — it looked like this was the purpose it was meant for. She shoved her gun in her pants and grabbed onto the pipe. She couldn't let them get her. She reached the top of the piping and reflexively pulled out her gun as she climbed onto the roof. She saw a figure in the distance.

"Brett, I can explain! Please, stop!" she yelled

loud enough to wake the dead, trying to be heard above the storm. The figure moved a bit. "Brett, let me help you!" She ran forward. The rain beat her face, blurring her vision. She heard the shot and felt it barely miss her. Then another. Her reflexes kicked in quicker than she could think. She flew to the ground and lifted the gun, firing twice before the lightning struck the building.

A few hours later, the firemen were just leaving. The lightning had caught the old roof on fire. Half of the building was demolished. Allie had slid down the drainpipe just in time. She had been nearly surrounded by flames when she realized she could do no more for Brett.

Randi walked up to her, putting a blanket over her shoulders. "Come on, kid," she said, putting an arm around Allie's shoulders. "We can finish up in the morning."

Allie looked up at her. "I killed her."

"They found a body — it'll take some work to identify it."

Allie wiped at the tears in her eyes and thought about the body she had seen removed. She had seen Brett's class ring on the charred finger that limply dropped off the stretcher. No one but Brett wore that ring. "She was going to retire."

"Hear it all the time."

"Kirsten was the one who killed them."

"If Brett was clean, she never woulda run."

"Leave me alone." Allie pulled away from Randi. Randi followed her for a few steps, but a reporter came to get a quote from her.

Splashing through the puddles, Allie walked through the rain, which was finally slowing down. She was alone, so very, very alone.

Epilogue

The coffin was lowered into the ground and the final prayers were said. Allie wiped her eyes and turned to go, wanting to leave before anyone started talking with her. She walked quickly, not really caring if she stepped in any puddles, not really caring whether or not she got drenched, not really caring about much at all.

Her mind wandered to Kirsten, the cause of several of the funerals she had been at, and thought about how to go about finding her, for she still had not been caught. She silently vowed to avenge Brett's death.

She looked up and saw Randi, standing with her back to Allie's car. Allie hoped the tears on her face looked like raindrops. The Detroit cop had been trying to reach her all week, but Allie would rather eat snake in the rain than have anything further to do with her.

"What do you want?"

"You okay?"

"No, I'm not okay. The woman that's killed most of the people I love is out there, free, and Brett is lying in that cold, damp, fucking ground. And it's all your fault."

"I didn't want Kirsten to get away."

"I don't know about that — all I know is you didn't want justice, you wanted Brett dead. Period." Allie turned to walk around the car.

"She killed my brother," Randi said, trying to stop Allie.

"Brett Higgins?"

"The last time Daniel was seen was at the Paradise Theater."

"He was hangin' around in that neighborhood and you think Brett killed him?"

"I know Brett killed him, or told somebody else to." Randi looked into Allie's eyes. "His body was found with the body of his best friend in a warehouse on Cass. They had both been shot after being in a fight. And I know he and his bud had a thing about a dancer named Storm."

"Brett didn't kill people for flirting or annoying her. If she did, Kirsten would have been buried five years ago and Brett would still be alive."

"Higgins killed Dan."

"Then he deserved it."

Randi stared at Allie. "Nobody deserves to die." She paused, as if to take the words back, but Allie hadn't missed the implications of what Randi had said.

"Listen to the omniscient God for she knows all," Allie said, taking a step toward Randi as anger flashed inside her. "The one time Brett ever killed anyone was the night they threatened and stalked Storm, broke into her house and tried to kill her."

"How do you know that?"

"She told me."

"She admitted killing someone and you didn't tell me?"

"Randi, fuck off. You got what you wanted, now leave me the fuck alone," Allie said, fleeing to the driver's side of the car.

"Allison, don't run from me."

"The only time I ever want to see your ugly face again is in a coffin." Allie climbed into her car, slammed the door and splashed Randi when she floored the accelerator.

Allie was oblivious to everything around her. She felt like she had been crying for days but, of course, that was because she had. It had only been truly embarrassing during the department's inquisition.

"You're crying, how sweet," a voice from behind her said. She almost swerved off the road in her fright.

One glance told her all she needed to know and, as her jaw dropped open, her uninvited guest climbed from the back seat and into the front.

"Keep driving," Brett said, pointing to the road.

"We don't want to make anyone suspicious, now, do we?"

Allie shook her head, trying to look at both the woman and at the road.

"Personally, I thought it was a rather bland service."

"You're alive."

"Now. But when I do kick, have me cremated and toss my ashes to the wind. Don't mess with any of this hoky bullshit."

"How . . . ?"

"The crematorium can handle most of it," Brett leaned back in the seat and lit a cigarette.

"I mean . . . Who . . . ?" Allie pointed back to the cemetery.

"Kirsten. She must've come to as you were chasing me. She climbed through Frankie's window — seeing as you had unlocked the door for her and all . . . I saw her and came up with this little plan."

"But . . ."

"I'm not sure if she was planning on killing me, or helping me escape from you, you little fiend, but anyway she got shot by you. Twice. In the head." Brett grinned. "I sat up there in the rain, without any time to think, and just prayed my aim was as good as I thought it was."

"I shot her, not you."

"Yeah, but I had to make you shoot her. It was me that fired at you. Let me tell you — I was real thankful for all those hours I spent at the firing range . . ."

"You shot at me?" Allie was dumbstruck.

"Twice! I was only surprised your reflexes didn't

take over sooner. I was pissed doin' it the first time, the second time I was scared shitless. I was hoping you'd shoot, and then they'd think you'd got me . . ."

"You set me up."

"Can you blame me? I mean, you didn't look like no angel that night yourself."

"So why're you here?"

"I think I can trust you. I've followed you since that night, and I know you resigned from the force . . ."

"But you and Kirsten don't look anything alike . . ."

"You take a couple of short-range shots in the head and see how wonderful you look."

"But fingerprints, dental charts . . ."

"The shots blew away her jaw, and the fire ate the rest of her up. The only ID she had on her was my credit cards and class ring. I was worried about it, but then that lightning bolt came . . ." She smoothed out her hair with her hand. "And I ran like hell." There was that grin again.

"What are you gonna do now?"

"First things first — pull over here." Brett pointed down a side street. When Allie stopped the car, Brett grabbed her and kissed her long and hard. Allie sighed. "Some things have just got to be done," Brett said with a smile. "But don't you ever kill me again."

Allie looked over at Brett and took her hand. "Once was enough."

"So I can trust you?"

Allie brushed the hair away from Brett's brown eyes. "A lifetime ago you told me that you just know when two souls meet."

"Forever and ever?"

"Forever and ever."

"If you go with me, you'll be stuck with me."

"I know," Allie said, kissing Brett's forehead, eyes and, finally, lips. A few moments later, when they finally parted, she looked deep into Brett's eyes. "I love you, Brett Higgins." Brett had the world's biggest shit ass grin on her face.

"Now, neither of us has much here anymore, so what's say we blow this popstand of a town and move to California, where the weather is so much better?"

"And what are we gonna do out there?"

"We don't have to do anything. We've got a trunk full of cash."

"What?"

"Well, I made a lot of money and didn't spend much. The cash in the trunk was what I kept at home. The rest is in Switzerland. Even if Frankie doesn't give me a dime for my parts of the businesses, we're still set for life."

"What about your house and car?"

"Left 'em to you in my will."

"Brett, dear, won't someone figure all this out?"

"Why and how? By the way, my name's not Brett — I am now Samantha Peterson. I always keep a spare identity handy for times like these. Frankie, Rick and I all kept spares in case anything ever came up."

Allie sat back and grinned. "Samantha?"

"Sam." Brett looked at her watch. "We'd better get a move on, our flight leaves at nine."

"You are something else."

"By the way, I forgot to thank you for coming to my funeral."

"It was the least I could do, after killing you and all."

LAST RITES by Tracey Richardson. 192 pp. 1st Stevie Houston mystery. ISBN 1-56280-164-3 11.95

EMBRACE IN MOTION by Karin Kallmaker. 256 pp. A whirlwind love affair. ISBN 1-56280-165-1 11.95

HOT CHECK by Peggy J. Herring. 192 pp. Will workaholic Alice fall for guitarist Ricky? ISBN 1-56280-163-5 11.95

OLD TIES by Saxon Bennett. 176 pp. Can Cleo surrender to a passionate new love? ISBN 1-56280-159-7 11.95

LOVE ON THE LINE by Laura DeHart Young. 176 pp. Will Stef win Kay's heart? ISBN 1-56280-162-7 11.95

DEVIL'S LEG CROSSING by Kaye Davis. 192 pp. 1st Maris Middleton mystery. ISBN 1-56280-158-9 11.95

COSTA BRAVA by Marta Balletbo Coll. 144 pp. Read the book, see the movie! ISBN 1-56280-153-8 11.95

MEETING MAGDALENE & OTHER STORIES by Marilyn Freeman. 144 pp. Read the book, see the movie! ISBN 1-56280-170-8 11.95

SECOND FIDDLE by Kate Calloway. 208 pp. P.I. Cassidy James' second case. ISBN 1-56280-169-6 11.95

LAUREL by Isabel Miller. 128 pp. By the author of the beloved *Patience and Sarah.* ISBN 1-56280-146-5 10.95

LOVE OR MONEY by Jackie Calhoun. 240 pp. The romance of real life. ISBN 1-56280-147-3 10.95

SMOKE AND MIRRORS by Pat Welch. 224 pp. 5th Helen Black Mystery. ISBN 1-56280-143-0 10.95

DANCING IN THE DARK edited by Barbara Grier & Christine Cassidy. 272 pp. Erotic love stories by Naiad Press authors. ISBN 1-56280-144-9 14.95

TIME AND TIME AGAIN by Catherine Ennis. 176 pp. Passionate love affair. ISBN 1-56280-145-7 10.95

PAXTON COURT by Diane Salvatore. 256 pp. Erotic and wickedly funny contemporary tale about the business of learning to live together. ISBN 1-56280-114-7 10.95

INNER CIRCLE by Claire McNab. 208 pp. 8th Carol Ashton Mystery. ISBN 1-56280-135-X 11.95

LESBIAN SEX: AN ORAL HISTORY by Susan Johnson. 240 pp. Need we say more? ISBN 1-56280-142-2 14.95

WILD THINGS by Karin Kallmaker. 240 pp. By the undisputed mistress of lesbian romance. ISBN 1-56280-139-2 11.95

THE GIRL NEXT DOOR by Mindy Kaplan. 208 pp. Just what you'd expect. ISBN 1-56280-140-6 11.95

NOW AND THEN by Penny Hayes. 240 pp. Romance on the westward journey. ISBN 1-56280-121-X 11.95

HEART ON FIRE by Diana Simmonds. 176 pp. The romantic and erotic rival of *Curious Wine.* ISBN 1-56280-152-X 11.95

DEATH AT LAVENDER BAY by Lauren Wright Douglas. 208 pp. 1st Allison O'Neil Mystery. ISBN 1-56280-085-X 11.95

YES I SAID YES I WILL by Judith McDaniel. 272 pp. Hot romance by famous author. ISBN 1-56280-138-4 11.95

FORBIDDEN FIRES by Margaret C. Anderson. Edited by Mathilda Hills. 176 pp. Famous author's "unpublished" Lesbian romance. ISBN 1-56280-123-6 21.95

SIDE TRACKS by Teresa Stores. 160 pp. Gender-bending Lesbians on the road. ISBN 1-56280-122-8 10.95

HOODED MURDER by Annette Van Dyke. 176 pp. 1st Jessie Batelle Mystery. ISBN 1-56280-134-1 10.95

WILDWOOD FLOWERS by Julia Watts. 208 pp. Hilarious and heart-warming tale of true love. ISBN 1-56280-127-9 10.95

NEVER SAY NEVER by Linda Hill. 224 pp. Rule #1: Never get involved with . . . ISBN 1-56280-126-0 10.95

THE SEARCH by Melanie McAllester. 240 pp. Exciting top cop Tenny Mendoza case. ISBN 1-56280-150-3 10.95

THE WISH LIST by Saxon Bennett. 192 pp. Romance through the years. ISBN 1-56280-125-2 10.95

FIRST IMPRESSIONS by Kate Calloway. 208 pp. P.I. Cassidy James' first case. ISBN 1-56280-133-3 10.95

OUT OF THE NIGHT by Kris Bruyer. 192 pp. Spine-tingling thriller. ISBN 1-56280-120-1 10.95

NORTHERN BLUE by Tracey Richardson. 224 pp. Police recruits Miki & Miranda — passion in the line of fire. ISBN 1-56280-118-X 10.95

LOVE'S HARVEST by Peggy J. Herring. 176 pp. by the author of *Once More With Feeling.* ISBN 1-56280-117-1 10.95

THE COLOR OF WINTER by Lisa Shapiro. 208 pp. Romantic love beyond your wildest dreams. ISBN 1-56280-116-3 10.95

FAMILY SECRETS by Laura DeHart Young. 208 pp. Enthralling romance and suspense. ISBN 1-56280-119-8 10.95

INLAND PASSAGE by Jane Rule. 288 pp. Tales exploring conventional & unconventional relationships. ISBN 0-930044-56-8 10.95

DOUBLE BLUFF by Claire McNab. 208 pp. 7th Carol Ashton Mystery. ISBN 1-56280-096-5 10.95

BAR GIRLS by Lauran Hoffman. 176 pp. See the movie, read the book! ISBN 1-56280-115-5 10.95

THE FIRST TIME EVER edited by Barbara Grier & Christine Cassidy. 272 pp. Love stories by Naiad Press authors. ISBN 1-56280-086-8 14.95

MISS PETTIBONE AND MISS McGRAW by Brenda Weathers. 208 pp. A charming ghostly love story. ISBN 1-56280-151-1 10.95

CHANGES by Jackie Calhoun. 208 pp. Involved romance and relationships. ISBN 1-56280-083-3 10.95

FAIR PLAY by Rose Beecham. 256 pp. 3rd Amanda Valentine Mystery. ISBN 1-56280-081-7 10.95

PAYBACK by Celia Cohen. 176 pp. A gripping thriller of romance, revenge and betrayal. ISBN 1-56280-084-1 10.95

THE BEACH AFFAIR by Barbara Johnson. 224 pp. Sizzling summer romance/mystery/intrigue. ISBN 1-56280-090-6 10.95

GETTING THERE by Robbi Sommers. 192 pp. Nobody does it like Robbi! ISBN 1-56280-099-X 10.95

FINAL CUT by Lisa Haddock. 208 pp. 2nd Carmen Ramirez Mystery. ISBN 1-56280-088-4 10.95

FLASHPOINT by Katherine V. Forrest. 256 pp. A Lesbian blockbuster! ISBN 1-56280-079-5 10.95

CLAIRE OF THE MOON by Nicole Conn. Audio Book —Read by Marianne Hyatt. ISBN 1-56280-113-9 16.95

FOR LOVE AND FOR LIFE: INTIMATE PORTRAITS OF LESBIAN COUPLES by Susan Johnson. 224 pp. ISBN 1-56280-091-4 14.95

DEVOTION by Mindy Kaplan. 192 pp. See the movie — read the book! ISBN 1-56280-093-0 10.95

SOMEONE TO WATCH by Jaye Maiman. 272 pp. 4th Robin Miller Mystery. ISBN 1-56280-095-7 10.95

GREENER THAN GRASS by Jennifer Fulton. 208 pp. A young woman — a stranger in her bed. ISBN 1-56280-092-2 10.95

TRAVELS WITH DIANA HUNTER by Regine Sands. Erotic lesbian romp. Audio Book (2 cassettes) ISBN 1-56280-107-4 16.95

CABIN FEVER by Carol Schmidt. 256 pp. Sizzling suspense and passion. ISBN 1-56280-089-1 10.95

THERE WILL BE NO GOODBYES by Laura DeHart Young. 192 pp. Romantic love, strength, and friendship. ISBN 1-56280-103-1 10.95

FAULTLINE by Sheila Ortiz Taylor. 144 pp. Joyous comic lesbian novel. ISBN 1-56280-108-2 9.95

OPEN HOUSE by Pat Welch. 176 pp. 4th Helen Black Mystery. ISBN 1-56280-102-3 10.95

ONCE MORE WITH FEELING by Peggy J. Herring. 240 pp. Lighthearted, loving romantic adventure. ISBN 1-56280-089-2 10.95

FOREVER by Evelyn Kennedy. 224 pp. Passionate romance — love overcoming all obstacles. ISBN 1-56280-094-9 10.95

WHISPERS by Kris Bruyer. 176 pp. Romantic ghost story ISBN 1-56280-082-5 10.95

NIGHT SONGS by Penny Mickelbury. 224 pp. 2nd Gianna Maglione Mystery. ISBN 1-56280-097-3 10.95

GETTING TO THE POINT by Teresa Stores. 256 pp. Classic southern Lesbian novel. ISBN 1-56280-100-7 10.95

PAINTED MOON by Karin Kallmaker. 224 pp. Delicious Kallmaker romance. ISBN 1-56280-075-2 11.95

THE MYSTERIOUS NAIAD edited by Katherine V. Forrest & Barbara Grier. 320 pp. Love stories by Naiad Press authors. ISBN 1-56280-074-4 14.95

DAUGHTERS OF A CORAL DAWN by Katherine V. Forrest. 240 pp. Tenth Anniversay Edition. ISBN 1-56280-104-X 11.95

BODY GUARD by Claire McNab. 208 pp. 6th Carol Ashton Mystery. ISBN 1-56280-073-6 11.95

CACTUS LOVE by Lee Lynch. 192 pp. Stories by the beloved storyteller. ISBN 1-56280-071-X 9.95

SECOND GUESS by Rose Beecham. 216 pp. 2nd Amanda Valentine Mystery. ISBN 1-56280-069-8 9.95

A RAGE OF MAIDENS by Lauren Wright Douglas. 240 pp. 6th Caitlin Reece Mystery. ISBN 1-56280-068-X 10.95

TRIPLE EXPOSURE by Jackie Calhoun. 224 pp. Romantic drama involving many characters. ISBN 1-56280-067-1 10.95

UP, UP AND AWAY by Catherine Ennis. 192 pp. Delightful romance. ISBN 1-56280-065-5 11.95

PERSONAL ADS by Robbi Sommers. 176 pp. Sizzling short stories. ISBN 1-56280-059-0 11.95

CROSSWORDS by Penny Sumner. 256 pp. 2nd Victoria Cross Mystery. ISBN 1-56280-064-7 9.95

SWEET CHERRY WINE by Carol Schmidt. 224 pp. A novel of suspense. ISBN 1-56280-063-9 9.95

CERTAIN SMILES by Dorothy Tell. 160 pp. Erotic short stories. ISBN 1-56280-066-3 9.95

EDITED OUT by Lisa Haddock. 224 pp. 1st Carmen Ramirez Mystery. ISBN 1-56280-077-9 9.95

WEDNESDAY NIGHTS by Camarin Grae. 288 pp. Sexy adventure. ISBN 1-56280-060-4 10.95

SMOKEY O by Celia Cohen. 176 pp. Relationships on the playing field. ISBN 1-56280-057-4 9.95

KATHLEEN O'DONALD by Penny Hayes. 256 pp. Rose and Kathleen find each other and employment in 1909 NYC. ISBN 1-56280-070-1 9.95

STAYING HOME by Elisabeth Nonas. 256 pp. Molly and Alix want a baby . . . or do they? ISBN 1-56280-076-0 10.95

TRUE LOVE by Jennifer Fulton. 240 pp. Six lesbians searching for love in all the "right" places. ISBN 1-56280-035-3 10.95

KEEPING SECRETS by Penny Mickelbury. 208 pp. 1st Gianna Maglione Mystery. ISBN 1-56280-052-3 9.95

THE ROMANTIC NAIAD edited by Katherine V. Forrest & Barbara Grier. 336 pp. Love stories by Naiad Press authors. ISBN 1-56280-054-X 14.95

UNDER MY SKIN by Jaye Maiman. 336 pp. 3rd Robin Miller Mystery. ISBN 1-56280-049-3. 11.95

CAR POOL by Karin Kallmaker. 272pp. Lesbians on wheels and then some! ISBN 1-56280-048-5 10.95

NOT TELLING MOTHER: STORIES FROM A LIFE by Diane Salvatore. 176 pp. Her 3rd novel. ISBN 1-56280-044-2 9.95

GOBLIN MARKET by Lauren Wright Douglas. 240pp. 5th Caitlin Reece Mystery. ISBN 1-56280-047-7 10.95

LONG GOODBYES by Nikki Baker. 256 pp. 3rd Virginia Kelly Mystery. ISBN 1-56280-042-6 9.95

FRIENDS AND LOVERS by Jackie Calhoun. 224 pp. Midwestern Lesbian lives and loves. ISBN 1-56280-041-8 11.95

BEHIND CLOSED DOORS by Robbi Sommers. 192 pp. Hot, erotic short stories. ISBN 1-56280-039-6 11.95

CLAIRE OF THE MOON by Nicole Conn. 192 pp. See the movie — read the book! ISBN 1-56280-038-8 10.95

SILENT HEART by Claire McNab. 192 pp. Exotic Lesbian romance. ISBN 1-56280-036-1 10.95

THE SPY IN QUESTION by Amanda Kyle Williams. 256 pp. 4th Madison McGuire Mystery. ISBN 1-56280-037-X 9.95

SAVING GRACE by Jennifer Fulton. 240 pp. Adventure and romantic entanglement. ISBN 1-56280-051-5 10.95

CURIOUS WINE by Katherine V. Forrest. 176 pp. Tenth Anniversary Edition. The most popular contemporary Lesbian love story. ISBN 1-56280-053-1 11.95

Audio Book (2 cassettes) ISBN 1-56280-105-8 16.95

CHAUTAUQUA by Catherine Ennis. 192 pp. Exciting, romantic adventure. ISBN 1-56280-032-9 9.95

A PROPER BURIAL by Pat Welch. 192 pp. 3rd Helen Black Mystery. ISBN 1-56280-033-7 9.95

SILVERLAKE HEAT: A Novel of Suspense by Carol Schmidt. 240 pp. Rhonda is as hot as Laney's dreams. ISBN 1-56280-031-0 9.95

LOVE, ZENA BETH by Diane Salvatore. 224 pp. The most talked about lesbian novel of the nineties! ISBN 1-56280-030-2 10.95

A DOORYARD FULL OF FLOWERS by Isabel Miller. 160 pp. Stories incl. 2 sequels to *Patience and Sarah.* ISBN 1-56280-029-9 9.95

MURDER BY TRADITION by Katherine V. Forrest. 288 pp. 4th Kate Delafield Mystery. ISBN 1-56280-002-7 11.95

THE EROTIC NAIAD edited by Katherine V. Forrest & Barbara Grier. 224 pp. Love stories by Naiad Press authors. ISBN 1-56280-026-4 14.95

DEAD CERTAIN by Claire McNab. 224 pp. 5th Carol Ashton Mystery. ISBN 1-56280-027-2 9.95

CRAZY FOR LOVING by Jaye Maiman. 320 pp. 2nd Robin Miller Mystery. ISBN 1-56280-025-6 10.95

STONEHURST by Barbara Johnson. 176 pp. Passionate regency romance. ISBN 1-56280-024-8 9.95

INTRODUCING AMANDA VALENTINE by Rose Beecham. 256 pp. 1st Amanda Valentine Mystery. ISBN 1-56280-021-3 10.95

UNCERTAIN COMPANIONS by Robbi Sommers. 204 pp. Steamy, erotic novel. ISBN 1-56280-017-5 11.95

A TIGER'S HEART by Lauren W. Douglas. 240 pp. 4th Caitlin Reece Mystery. ISBN 1-56280-018-3 9.95

PAPERBACK ROMANCE by Karin Kallmaker. 256 pp. A delicious romance. ISBN 1-56280-019-1 10.95

THE LAVENDER HOUSE MURDER by Nikki Baker. 224 pp. 2nd Virginia Kelly Mystery. ISBN 1-56280-012-4 9.95

PASSION BAY by Jennifer Fulton. 224 pp. Passionate romance, virgin beaches, tropical skies. ISBN 1-56280-028-0 10.95

STICKS AND STONES by Jackie Calhoun. 208 pp. Contemporary lesbian lives and loves. ISBN 1-56280-020-5 9.95
Audio Book (2 cassettes) ISBN 1-56280-106-6 16.95

UNDER THE SOUTHERN CROSS by Claire McNab. 192 pp. Romantic nights Down Under. ISBN 1-56280-011-6 11.95

GRASSY FLATS by Penny Hayes. 256 pp. Lesbian romance in the '30s. ISBN 1-56280-010-8 9.95

These are just a few of the many Naiad Press titles — we are the oldest and largest lesbian/feminist publishing company in the world. We also offer an enormous selection of lesbian video products. Please request a complete catalog. We offer personal service; we encourage and welcome direct mail orders from individuals who have limited access to bookstores carrying our publications.